The Diligent Bugs of Kook Bog

The Diligent Bugs of Kook Bog

A.J. Mullen

Illustrations by Abe Ong

Safflower Press, Vashon, WA
2017

Cover art by Abe Ong

Insect illustrations courtesy geesucks.deviantart.com

First Printing: 2017

ISBN: 978-0-578-18944-4

For H & B

Chapter 1
The Day the Ground Gave Way

YOUNG RUDY PROMOVENDIS was fourteen years old when his world, quite literally, collapsed.

It came as a surprise to him, but the signs had been there all along. The mud had been rising throughout Mossville for months, if not years, and the periodic rumbles of the shifting earth had become all too familiar to the town's residents. From time to time, Rudy heard the hushed talk among adults of a coming catastrophe. There had already been damage from smaller quakes and slides. Mud-related mishaps had even claimed a handful of lives, but the incidents had been isolated. The worst, it was rightly feared by many, was yet to come.

Rudy's father had certainly sensed the danger. Pythagorus Promovendis had been more preoccupied by the encroaching mud than anybody else. The older man's eyes shone with a strange, mad fire when the soft ground groaned beneath their feet. His father knew that time was short to prepare.

But for Rudy, the reality of the threat had not sunk in.

On the fateful morning Rudy had opened his window in preparation for an experiment involving Pyrolusite powder and spirits of salt.

Even in his youth, Rudy was cautious and conscientious scientist.

He pushed the window up as high as it went and drew the curtains back to let in as much fresh air as he could. This wasn't Rudy's first time working with hazardous gasses and he had no wish to extinguish *himself* in the name of science.

Below the window, through the orange and yellow autumn leaves still clinging to their branches, his father's work shed stood quietly, embedded in the soft mud of the hillside. Rudy's gaze lingered on the work shed. Once upon a time, his father had welcomed his help, but as Rudy got older, his father had become cagey and distant. Rudy had not seen the inside of the work shed since he was seven or eight years old. The rejection stung. He knew his father was working on something extraordinary.

"The less you know about my work these days the better," his father had told him. "The time will come. Wait."

But Rudy found it impossible not to wonder. His father's occasional, tantalizing outbursts made his curiosity burn all the more hotly.

When I finish my work, all of this will be behind us," Pythagorus mumbled from time to time over yet another supper of thin porridge and offal. "This family's troubles will be over, along with all of Mossville's."

But when Rudy pressed him for more on the nature of the windfall, his father became gruff and evasive.

"In due time, boy," he said. But the time had never come.

Rudy returned to his experiment. An ancient leather-bound tome lay on his desk, tied around the middle with a bone-white ribbon. *Principia Chemica* was printed in faded gold leaf across the cover. Rudy untied the ribbon and gently opened the book.

A stiff wire stand held a test tube a few feet above the surface of his desk. Rudy spooned the black powder into the test tube and poured the clear liquid after it. He struck a match and lit the wick of a small alcohol burner. A low flame began to glow.

A curl of greenish-yellow gas began to rise from the test tube. Rudy sat back pulled his shirt in front of his face instinctively as the faint whiff of the gas—somewhere between pepper and pineapple—reached his nose.

"Rudolph!" his mother's voice came up through the floorboards.

Rudy blew out the flame and scurried to the head of the stairs.

"Yes, Mother!" he called.

"Wood!" said his mother.

"Yes, Mother!"

Quickly, Rudy put on his boots and jacket and went out to the woodpile behind the house. He took the ax from its place against the pile and split three logs, as much as he could carry.

8

As he gathered the woods in his arms, he heard a faint buzzing sound. He looked around.

A loose cloud of aphids had begun to take shape amid the trees behind the house. Rudy watched as the cloud thickened and grew. Slowly, the aphids began to rise. Rudy's gaze followed the pulsating swarm of aphids upward.

With a start, Rudy realized that other insects had also begun to swarm and rise. Throughout the woods, columns of flies and gnats emerged in ragged vertical streaks. As he watched, the streaks moved together, consolidating into a dark column which extended straight into the sky.

Rudy clutched the bundle of wood and ran into the house.

In the kitchen, Rudy's mother was fiddling with the door of the stove. She was a large woman with thick, strong hands. The latch of the door flopped uselessly in her fingers and the door swung freely on its hinge.

"Where is your father? He said he'd fix this when he came home from town, but that was hours ago!"

Piece by piece, she took the wood from Rudy's arms and tossed it into the belly of the stove.

"He must have come home and gone straight to that work shed of his," she said. "He has no sense of time in there."

"The bugs are acting strangely again, Mother," said Rudy.

His mother paused, knitting her brows.

"Go on up to your room," she said. "I'll call you when your broth is hot."

"Mother," he said. "What do you suppose Father is building?"

Rudy's mother sighed.

"I don't know, Rudolph," she said. "But for all his quirks, your father is a brilliant man. If he says his work is important, I believe that it is. I'm sure he has his reasons for his secrecy."

Rudy shrugged, unsatisfied with the answer.

Rudy returned to his room and sat quietly for a time. He found a scarf in the bottom of his chest of clothing and wrapped it around his face before returning to his experiment. Once again, he positioned the burner underneath the test tube and lit the wick. Once again, the greenish gas began to snake upward.

Rudy felt a tremor pass through him. It was so subtle that for a moment he thought he had merely shivered, although he did not feel cold. Rudy paused. For a second or two, all was still. Then came another tremor. The burner on the table rattled, then went silent for two or three more seconds.

That was all the warning there was.

Before Rudy could even stand, the floor beneath him lurched sickeningly. His stomach rose as his body dropped and the floor bumped to a halt, hurling him off of his chair, then shifted and began to creak in the opposite direction, like a ship on a stormy sea.

The contents of Rudy's desk, burner, test tube, books, and all spilled onto the floor with a crash. Rudy gasped as he watched the poisonous green puff rise from the shattered test tube. The burner, too, had smashed. In an instant, a low flame flashed across the floor, where the alcohol from the burner was spreading slowly.

Rudy leaped to his feet. He grabbed the tattered woolen blanket from his bed and began to beat the burning alcohol. The blue flames danced and licked the blanket. He held his breath and squinted his eyes against the spreading haze of chlorine that was filling his room. From below he heard his mother's shout.

"Goodness! The stove!"

The flames began to subside under Rudy's beating. He threw the blanket over the remaining alcohol and stomped it out completely with his feet. The green gas, too, was thinning in the wind from the open window. The room's movement slowed and eventually shuddered to a halt with the floor still at a sickening angle.

Rudy's relief was short-lived.

The room was uncomfortably hot. And when dared to gasp for air through his tightly wadded shirt, the acrid smell of smoke filled his nostrils. Only moments before, the wisps of smoke from below had been barely noticeable. Now thick gray tendrils seeped through the cracks between the floorboards and under his door. Rudy realized sickly that the real fire had been beneath him the whole time.

Rudy dashed to the door of his bedroom, but the doorknob burned his fingers and he pulled away. Beyond his bedroom the crackling of the flames and the creaking of burning wood told him that the blaze was advancing rapidly through the house. Smoke now billowed into his room from all directions.

There was only one way out. It would not be an easy jump, but not impossible. He sprinted across the floor of his bedroom, through the smoke and lingering green gas, and dove headlong out the window into the branches of the maple outside.

As the branches bent beneath him, Rudy looked back at the room he'd just escaped. At that moment his mother, panting and soot-blackened, burst into the bedroom door at the far side of his room, followed by a billow of flame.

"Mother!" he screamed, as the branches gave way, rolling him onto the soft ground below with a belching splat. The mud at the base of the house was nearly up to his knees.

Rudy struggled to stand. The house was an inferno. He looked up desperately at his own bedroom window, but his mother did not appear.

He spun around and began down the slope towards his father's work shed. The hill had become a nearly solid mudslide. Trees and bushes seemed to crawl alongside him like slugs as he splashed and slid into the deepening muck.

"Father!" he cried. "Father! Help!"

But as he approached the place where the work shed should have been, he felt first confusion and then raw horror. When he finally spotted the corner of the work shed's roof poking up from the soupy mud, his heart stopped.

"FATHER!" he screamed.

He stood waist deep in the oozing river of mud. Above him the fire roared, consuming his home and all he had ever known. Below him the remnants of his father's precious work shed disappeared into the brown deluge.

"Father!" his voice was now only a rasp.

It had all happened so suddenly that his emotions could scarcely catch up to the horrific events. His head spun. His parents were gone. His home was gone. Everything was gone.

The mud of Mossville had claimed its latest victims. The day would stay with Rudy all his life. He would carry the burden of the events even into adulthood. When his own son Theo was born, Rudy had to glance away in pain for a moment at the reflection of his parents in the bright-eyed baby's face.

At least Mossville was safe now, he told himself. At least his child would never know what it was to fear and distrust the very ground upon which he stood.

He had no idea how wrong he was.

Chapter 2
The Noble Gnat Lends a Hand

THE MOTH'S POWDERY WINGS sparkled golden and gray in the dim light of the old bulb overhead. Theo Promovendis held its body gingerly between the tips of his fingers. Getting them into the harnesses was the most difficult part. This one was the last. Theo sucked his lip in concentration as he placed the moth's body into the delicate wire structure, carefully inserting each leg into its place. A fine, dark thread ran from the harness. Theo snapped the tiny latch across the moth's midsection and released the moth to join the mass of others fluttering above his desk. Each one was tethered to the complex mechanical apparatus laid out across the desktop.

Although it was daytime, the light from the bulb was the only illumination in Theo's bedroom aside from a narrow crack at the edge of his curtains. His father often complained that he should spend more time outside in the sunlight, but that couldn't be helped. After all, it was only because of his father's annoying rules that Theo was forced to work in such secrecy in the first place.

The room was strewn with the makings of countless projects. Parts and pulleys, springs and sprockets, bulbs, tubes and bearings covered the floor and sat in piles in the corners of the room. Theo was always finding discarded little mechanical treasures around town, particularly in the mother lode of the Mossville Municipal Dump. At least, the things he found had *mostly* been discarded. On the occasions when Theo borrowed items that were (strictly speaking) still in use, it was always with the earnest intention to return them as soon as he was finished with them. But of course, the work of such a restless young inventor was never truly finished.

There were other things in the room more typical of a boy of eleven. There were models of airplanes, ships and trains in various states of completion. Vehicles made of balsa wood, cloth, paper and tin were scattered on the shelves of the bookcase and displayed atop the wardrobe and the large antique cabinet.

On the bookshelf, among comic books and hobby magazines, stood several imposing tomes. Among the books were *The Boy's Anthology of Tales of High Adventure*, *Braustache & Bakerfield's Illustrated Encyclopedia of Mechanical Movements and Assemblies*, *The Comprehensive Guide to the Design and Construction of Lifelike Clockwork Automata*, and *Waldo Malone's How To Build Your Own Analytical Engine with Odds And Ends From Around the House*. In the corner beside the bookshelf lay more books concealed under blankets, newspaper comics pages, and hand-drawn blueprints. The worn bindings of *The Young Outdoorsman's Field Guide to The Noble Gnat and His Habitats*, *Physics for the Amateur Horticulturist* and *Bullock and Brewster's Compendium of Arthropod Semiochemical Interactions* peeked out from under the coverings, which hid the pile of books a little too well to have been placed entirely by accident.

Theo glanced once over his shoulder at the door and sat still for a few seconds, listening for any sounds from outside the room. He quietly opened the doors of the cabinet and took out an old wooden trunk. He set it on the corner of his desk and opened it with a tarnished brass key.

The trunk was packed to the brim with jars and vials. An apothecary scale and weights were tucked into one corner. Droppers, measuring spoons, and tweezers were wedged between containers of variously colored powders and fluids.

On his forehead Theo wore a pair of bulky, riveted brass aviation goggles with darkly mirrored lenses that, he had been told, had once belonged to his grandfather. He brought them down over his eyes.

He took a jar containing a bright orange liquid from the trunk and placed it upon the desk. He twisted the lid and it opened with a pop. A shudder passed through the fluttering cloud of moths above the desk, and their movements seemed to take on a new urgency. He took out a small leather pouch and tugged it open to reveal a few teaspoons of flax-colored powder. With a tiny

14

medicine spoon and a dropper he set to work preparing the mechanical apparatus that glinted dimly between the shadows of the moths.

The apparatus comprised four steel rods covered with a network of small copper gutters. At the narrower end was a jumble of much shorter and narrower rods, joints, and wires.

The two halves of the apparatus were connected by a large hinge. A mechanism of fine metal cables and pulleys enabled bending at the joint. Along the lengths of the rods were hundreds of tiny, hinged platforms. From each of the platforms, hoses no thicker than spaghetti emerged to join the gutters. At intervals along the machine, raised reservoirs were connected to clear tubes. Several larger basins jutted at odd angles near the wider end of the machine. A coil of brass tubing wormed down the length of the machine into the tangle of parts at the narrow end.

With the medicine spoon, Theo placed small piles of the flax-colored powder onto the platforms. He glanced at a tattered notebook filled with scrawled diagrams and equations. Not every platform received the same amount of powder, and some received none at all. To some of the platforms, he added a drop of dark brown fluid with a dropper. To others he sprinkled a pinch of bone white powder. He squeezed a drop of whitish liquid into each of the reservoirs.

He had calculated the amounts of the ingredients precisely. Any deviation would ruin the execution of his program. He held his breath as he leaned over his work. He did not have enough of the flax-colored pollen to waste. A sneeze could set him back weeks.

At length, he finished. A complex pattern of yellowish, whitish and brownish piles dotted the platform assembly of the machine.

Theo reached into the cabinet and withdrew two cube-shaped plywood boxes, each with three round holes cut in each side. The holes were covered with a fine mesh screen. On each of the boxes a label was affixed. One of them read BLACK GNATS and the other read BOG APHIDS. An almost imperceptible buzzing sound emanated from inside each of the boxes, but the tones were different. Together, they composed a sound not unlike the hum of electricity.

Timing was of the essence in the next step. Once the gnats and aphids began their circuits, he would only have few moments to introduce the leonore extract and activate the moths. The substance had a powerful effect on all the bugs, and leaving it exposed could have disastrous results.

He slid the lid of the first box open and a wisp of gnats curled out into the room. The swarm darkened and expanded over the desk, mingling with the moths.

Theo opened the second box and a bright green cloud of aphids emerged. The aphids were bigger than the gnats and the movement of the swarm was less delicate. They too collected above the desk, adding swirls of green to the expanding cloud.

The gnats were already responding to the powder. Theo watched as fine trails of gnats curled towards the platforms of the machine. One by one they struck their targets. A tiny click sounded each time a wisp of gnats struck a hinged platform, flipping it like a switch. The clicks came more rapidly. As combinations of the platform-switches were thrown, tiny valves on the hoses began to open and close, releasing the whitish fluid from the reservoirs. As the whitish fluid started to flow, the aphids reacted.

Soon the aphids flew in a bright green blur through the tubes along the length of the machine. The clicking sped to a stuttering hum.

Theo brought out a wooden honey dipper. He dipped the end into the jar of leonore extract and stirred it around. He withdrew a deep pink ball of the glistening, sticky substance.

With deft movements, he passed the dipper over each of the jutting basins, letting a single gooey drop fall into each of them. Then he quickly replaced the lid of the leonore jar.

The leonore flowed into the system. A faint odor arose as it came into contact with the whitish fluid. It smelled like sweet, burnt cloves. The moths shot to the ends of their tethers like spores on the head of a dandelion, then dove into action.

The movement of the moths was deliberate and complex. They flew in a tightly choreographed dance, their tethers braiding and unbraiding repeatedly. The tethers tugged at tiny spindles. They popped switches open just as other moths struck them shut. They pushed bolts into housings and snapping them back out. A clattering racket rose over the hum of the gnats and the whirr of the aphids.

The tangle of tubes, wires and rods at the narrow end of the apparatus twitched. Theo cautiously raised his goggles to get a better look.

The knot of parts twitched again and began to loosen. Slowly, with jitters and jerks, the bundle began to unfold like a strange mechanical flower blooming. Theo stared.

Suddenly, it snapped open into the shape of a hand, with fingers and thumb fully extended.

Theo's eyes widened as he watched the movements of the mechanical hand. Blurry green veins of aphids coursed through the fine brass pipework of the fingers. The flanged knuckles bent and straightened jerkily, responding to rods in the forearm. These in turn were driven by the complex interactions of the moths.

Theo took a porous, gray stone from the trunk. A tremor rippled through the swarm of moths. He brought the stone closer to the twitching, skeletal hand.

With a sudden and deliberate motion, the hand grasped the stone. Theo stepped back. The hand continued to grip the stone. A smile of satisfaction crept across Theo's face. This was it.

"Theo!" came his father's voice.

Theo froze for a second then scrambled in all directions at once, knocking the trunk off the desk and spilling its contents all over the floor. The bugs went wild. Aphids and gnats fell out of formation and filled the room.

"Wait!" Theo blurted. "I'm coming!"

"Where are you?" called his father from down the hall.

There was no time to try to collect the bugs. Theo dashed to the window and flung it open. He swung his arms frantically to clear the room.

"Coming dad!"

His father's footsteps approached. The gnats and aphids hung in lazy clouds throughout the room. Theo grabbed a blanket from his bed and whipped it wildly, sending the bugs into swirling eddies around the room.

The door cracked open. Theo grabbed the mechanical arm and flung it to the floor beneath his desk, moths and all. He swung the blanket in one last wide arc through the air and threw it over the mess of bottles, moths and machinery at his feet. A tattered cloud of aphids and gnats still hung inside the window. The door opened fully and they dispersed in a puff as Rudy Promovendis peeked into the room.

"Theo?"

Rudy was a tall, thin man with a shock of bright red hair even more unkempt and willful than his son's and an enormous, bushy mustache to match it. Like his son's, his eyes were green and sharp, though they had a greater tendency to wander as their owner became lost in thought. Theo had often wondered whether his own ability to focus on one thing at a time had been the one trait he had inherited from his late mother.

Rudy held a crumpled bundle of blueprints in one hand and a pencil in the other. He scribbled notes as he nudged the door open with his shoulder.

"Ready to go?" he said without looking up.

"Go?" Theo tried to slow his breathing. The last of the gnats disappeared just as Rudy raised his head.

"To help me with the harvester. Don't you remember?" said Rudy.

"You said we'd do that Saturday!" Theo said.

"Saturday?" Rudy's eyes drifted downward in thought and he sucked on the end of his mustache. "Isn't it Saturday today?"

"No, dad, it's Friday. And there's the festival in town!" said Theo.

"Ah," said Rudy. "I guess I meant Friday then. We'd better get to it while it's still early!"

"What about the festival?" said Theo.

"All the more reason not to dawdle!" said Rudy, turning to leave. "I'll be waiting up at the shelter."

Theo was about to complain when he heard a loud tap above his head. One of the moths was banging against the light bulb, its long black tether dangling free.

Rudy stopped in the doorway and slowly turned back around to face the room. Theo grabbed the tether and pulled the moth behind his back, hoping his father hadn't noticed.

Rudy sniffed at the air and looked around.

"Say, you haven't been into my pollens have you?" he said.

Theo stared blankly.

"Me?"

Rudy's brows knitted for a moment.

"Hmm," he said, then turned back to the door, his attention turning back to the bundle of blueprints. "Chop chop!"

Chapter 3
The Charge of the Marvelous
Bug-Driven Harvester

THE SHELTER WAS ABOUT FIVE feet high and built from branches and leaves, with a U-shaped foundation of dirt and stones. It was effective both as camouflage and at protecting its contents from the worst of the elements. Looking from the nearby road, nobody would have imagined there might be anything there besides woods. But hidden in the shelter was a great deal more indeed.

By the time Theo arrived, Rudy had already pulled away most of the shelter. A large, strangely shaped object lay in the clearing about six feet wide, ten feet long, and nearly the height of the shelter itself. The object was entirely wrapped in canvas and oilcloth tarps and bound with ropes.

"I don't see why you don't just keep it in the shed," said Theo.

"When the patent comes though, I'll be able to keep it right out in the open for all to see," said Rudy. "And boy, will they be happy to see it! In the meantime though… hand me that rope will you?"

Rudy slid two long wooden poles under the object and lashed them in place.

"The amount of work this will save people," Rudy began. "That's the important thing, son! To give people something they can use!"

Theo looked skeptically at his father.

"Mark my words son," said Rudy. "You do that, and you'll never be lonely!"

"I'm not lonely anyway," said Theo.

Rudy smiled at Theo. There was a trace of sadness in his smile.

"We've got to get this to Gurwell's field before it gets dark," he said. "You get in back."

Theo took his place at the rear of the object. They both bent down and grasped the poles.

"Heave ho!" cried Rudy. They lifted the object with all of their strength.

It was all they could do to keep the burden off the ground as they hauled it out of the woods and down the road. Rudy led the way, gripping a pole in each fist and straining forward so hard that the curve of his shoulders seemed to disappear altogether, leaving an almost unbroken line from his neck to his wrists.

Theo quickly gave up on one of the poles. He put all his effort into shouldering the pole on his right, leaving the pole on the left to plow a deep rut into the dirt of the road. The pair advanced haltingly towards the broad hillside field a mile and a half down the road.

In addition to the tarp-covered object they bore between them, Rudy and Theo each carried baggage of their own. Rudy wore a high, top-heavy rucksack piled high with pouches, boxes, and shelves. Brightly colored bottles dangled from hooks on the pack frame. Theo carried a worn leather shoulder bag covered with pockets and pouches. It bumped awkwardly against his knees with every step he took.

"I'm dying!" Theo cried.

"Legs bent, back straight!" Rudy called back between clenched teeth. The veins of his neck bulged like sausages. "You'll be fine!"

Theo could only grunt in reply.

At last, Rudy and Theo came to the spot where the road split. One fork switched back and led further down the hill—eventually to the town of Mossville proper—and the other disappeared into a broad, gently-sloping field of barley. The far edge of the field ended abruptly at a cliff. Far beyond could be seen the jagged ridge of a deep ravine, hazy in the distance.

The late afternoon sky was just beginning to pinken and the sun cast a warm golden glow over the field.

Theo spun around dramatically and collapsed onto his back in the tall green barley.

"I'm dead!" he gasped.

Rudy had already begun untying the cords. He tossed the tarps aside to reveal the harvester.

By the standards of such machines, it was very small, making the revolving reaper apparatus at its front look outsized and all the more menacing. Rows of shiny blades meshed with each other like a system of gears.

The rest of the machine was no less remarkable. At first glance, it looked like a heap of junk bristling with shafts, hoses, and pipes. Tangled tufts of wiring peeked out from every cranny, and the surface of the machine was covered with platforms and hinges that looked like a catastrophic collision of clarinets.

But there was nothing haphazard about Rudy's creation.

Theo turned his head from where he lay in the barley. He eyed his father's machine. The mechanisms were all familiar. Theo knew much more than his father realized about the work-ings of the machine.

Nevertheless, it was impressive. It was the industrial-strength big sibling of Theo's own creations.

"You gonna come back to life and give me a hand?" called Rudy.

Rudy wedged one of the poles under the contraption and po-sitioned a large rock under the pole to form a lever. Theo climbed to his feet.

"I'll lift," said Rudy. "You get the legs out."

Rudy bore down on the lever and the mountain of machinery lifted enough for Theo to reach beneath it. Theo crawled down and withdrew a heavy segmented appendage that had been folded under the machine. There were three of these on each side of the machine. Rudy and Theo extracted them one by one. When they finished, Theo set about untangling a mess of hydraulic hoses and connecting them to the legs. Rudy affixed a huge, balloon-shaped canvas bag to a metal ring at the back end of the machine. When it was all assembled the machine looked very much like an enor-mous mechanical tick.

A large crow landed on a branch of a nearby tree. It eyed the father and son and their peculiar contraption curiously.

Rudy stepped back from the harvester and sniffed the air. It was time to prime the device.

Rudy rummaged through his pack and withdrew a small stack of very thin hinged boards bundled with canvas straps. He unfolded the boards to form a handy wearable workbench. Theo helped him get his shoulders through the straps and buckle himself in. The workbench was composed of a tabletop that extended all the way around his midsection. From the tabletop extended vertical supports which held three columns of shelves and pigeon-holes, an angled writing surface and inkwell, a vice grip, and a collection of adjustable mechanical arms. The arms supported variously-sized clamps, clips and cup-holders. As with his back-pack, the precarious appearance of the wearable workbench be-lied its sturdiness and reliability.

With Theo's help, Rudy stocked the clips and clamps of the workbench with jars and canisters from his pack. Theo handed them to Rudy one by one: lyophilized royal jelly powder, ground tetrastigma root resin, mealybug honeydew, extract of Karner Blue butterfly mating pheromone.

"You gonna do the whole field?" asked Theo.

"As much as we can get to," said Rudy.

"Don't you think you should tell Mr. Gurwell first?"

Rudy shook his head and waved his hand dismissively.

"He'll be glad to have it done!" he said. "Who wouldn't? Now, set up the bellows while I prime this fella."

Theo looked out over the field. He turned to his father's ruck-sack to find a large bellows made of wood and leather, a wooden tripod, and a broad iron pan. He set the bellows up so its nozzle was supported by the tripod and then affixed the pan to the noz-zle.

Rudy's wearable workbench was fully stocked with gels, flu-ids, and powders. He climbed onto the machine and got to work priming it. He worked quickly. He dusted the platforms on the back of the machine with pollens and pheromone powders. He filled up hoppers and basins with variously colored fluids. At last, he produced a large vial of glistening, deep pink leonore extract and poured it into the flanged brass pipe-ends protruding from the machine. The leonore extract flowed into the workings of the ma-chine, mingling with the other ingredients.

Rudy jumped down and unstrapped his wearable workbench.

"Get ready, son!"

"Dad?"

"One, two…"

"Dad!" said Theo.

"What is it?" said Rudy.

Theo held a bottle of whitish fluid.

"What?"

Theo looked up at his father.

"It's just," he hesitated, "this looks like it's starting to crystal-lize. That will… I mean, won't that be bad for the aphids?"

Rudy knitted his brow and gave a puzzled smile.

"Good boy!" he said. "Taking an interest!"

"But—" Theo began, but his father cut him off.

"The aphids will be fine!" shouted Rudy. He poured a cup of leonore extract into the pan affixed to the bellows. He bore down on the handle. The gusts of air turned slightly pink as they passed over the leonore.

After five good, strong bursts, Rudy disconnected the pan and emptied the remainder of its contents into a hopper on the side of the harvester.

Theo watched the pale pink of the attractant disperse into the light breeze. All was quiet, save for the rustling barley. Theo and Rudy stood motionless in anticipation, Rudy tense and eager, Theo wincing with trepidation. For several long minutes, nothing happened.

Rudy and Theo squinted into the distance far beyond the cliff edge of the field, beyond even the valley below. They stared in-tently in the direction of the hazy edge of the distant ravine. As they watched, something in the quality of the haze began to change. Almost imperceptibly at first, but more distinctly with each passing moment, the haze began to darken. A black cloud was forming over the edge of the ravine.

Rudy nodded.

"Here we go," he said. "Stand back."

The cloud continued to grow and darken. It extended upward over the valley. It rose slowly into the sky and began to arch towards them like a great, blurry, black rainbow.

At first, the sound was scarcely distinguishable from the breeze over the field. In time it became a low hum, faint but clearly audible. The hum grew louder as the cloud spread overhead, darkening the sky.

Now the cloud was close enough to distinguish it for what it was: a great, swarming mass of insects. They filled the sky now, describing a smeared parabola over the valley below.

As many times as Theo had seen this process unfold, it always took his breath away when the bugs hit.

The bugs hit now.

In an instant, the hum grew to a deafening roar as the massive swarm impacted the ground like a meteor striking down. Rudy and Theo covered their faces and ducked instinctively, buffeted by the force of the swarm. All at once the machine was engulfed in a chaotic, buzzing blur.

Seen from up close, the swarm of insects was not solid black at all. It was a dark, swirling mix of black, brown, and green, dotted and streaked with red, purple, orange, and yellow. A glimpse of glowing blue-green phosphorus appeared in its depths. Here and there clusters of yellow sparks twinkled like stars in writhing, grainy nebulae.

No sooner had the swarm crashed down upon the machine than the elaborate chemical preparations began to take effect. Like clockwork, the bugs began to separate and take their places in the workings of the harvester. Green aphids split into blurred streams and shot into the brass circulatory system of the machine. Clouds of gnats collected into crackling masses over banks of tiny switches. Moths and butterflies snapped themselves into harnesses to bring the mechanical hulk alive.

And come alive it did. Switches clicked. Clutches caught. Cogs connected. The sound began as a chaotic clatter but soon sped to a smooth purr. The mechanical beast began to stir.

Still waving stray midges and aphids from their eyes, Rudy and Theo stood back and watched the machine transform into something very much like a living creature. It rose slowly on its six legs. The twisting lattice of blades across its front rotated faster and faster. The blades glinted like a steely grin.

At its full height, the back of the machine rose to almost ten feet in the air. The spinning blades stayed low and flush with the surface of the sloping field. The huge bag at the rear of the machine ballooned out as the first cuttings of barley flew. It began to walk. The pattern of its six-legged steps was identical to that of an insect. Slowly, the monstrous mechanical harvester advanced into the field, mowing into its first broad swath of barley.

Rudy grinned and gave his son a thumbs up sign.

Theo pricked up his ears. For a moment, he wondered if he was being oversensitive. Something sounded amiss within the workings. It was a clatter or knock of some kind, barely audible. It could have been the transmission, or perhaps it was the rack-and-pinion system for leveling the blade. But something was clearly—

"Dad!" called Theo, but it was no use to shout. Rudy was walking slowly backwards in front of the machine, as though coaxing it along. He was well out of earshot amid the deafening rumble of the machine. He seemed unaware of the increasingly erratic knocks emitting from the bowels of the machine.

Suddenly, something went very wrong. With a thunderous crack, a burst of insects exploded from the center of the machine. The smooth circulatory motion of the aphids kicked into an insane pattern of jittery, jumping streaks. The machine shuddered and shook, momentarily stopping in its tracks.

Rudy could see that something was wrong now. He reached into his jacket pocket and withdrew what appeared to be a perfume spritzer. He raised it towards the machine.

"Dad, no!" cried Theo, but his voice could not rise above the din.

Rudy squeezed the ball of the spritzer and sent a puff of clear fluid in the direction of the machine. But the effect was not what he expected. Rather than being calmed, the cloud of bugs grew even more wild and spread even further beyond the edges of the machine. Smears of color flew in jerks and spasms amid the knotted black and green swarms. The tethers driving the harvester twisted and tangled.

The machine reared up and dove forward, its spinning blade plunging into the ground just inches from Rudy's feet. Rudy leaped away and began to run, firing off a few more spritzes of fluid in a panic.

The large crow that had been watching the scene from the nearby tree took flight, but it did not fly far. A clump of hard earth shot up from the harvester's blade and struck it full in the breast. The crow's wings folded over its head and it dropped like a stone.

The machine pulled its blade from the ground and jolted forward. It charged after Rudy, who was now running away at full speed, knees high. He squirted the little spritzer helplessly over his shoulder.

The machine moved in jerks and fits but its legs were long. In a few wobbly six-legged staggers it was nearly upon Rudy. Its deadly blades were a spinning helix of knives. It reared high in the air.

Theo tore into his father's pack and flung its contents out in a panic. At last he found what he was looking for. He pulled out a jar of white powder.

Rudy looked over his shoulder to get a better shot with the spritzer but the angle was awkward and he stumbled over his own feet, landing hard on his elbow. The harvester loomed above him, its madly whizzing blades poised to plunge down and slice him to ribbons. Rudy clenched his eyes shut.

Theo gripped the jar of powder. There was no time for measuring, no time for the bellows and pan. He lobbed the jar at the machine with all his might. It struck its target dead on. A puff of white emerged from the guts of the harvester.

At once the aphids began to disperse. Soon the gnats and midges followed. In only moments all of the insects had loosened their grip on the machinery. The clouds of bugs blurred and thinned. Green streams eddied and dissipated. Moths and butterflies released themselves from their harnesses and fluttered away. The machinery spun down and the limbs of the beast went lax.

Rudy pulled himself out of the way just as the blade of the harvester collapsed into the ground.

The bugs had abandoned the machine. They flew into the air over the field and the valley below. Clumps of insects still buzzed and small, patchy rabbles hung in the air over the barley. A figure eight of green aphids rose into the darkening sky, blurring at the edges.

Theo ran to where Rudy lay on the ground.

"Are you okay?" he asked.

"Darn aphids!" said Rudy to himself. He paused, then looked at his son. "How did you know?"

Theo shook his head.

"Just a lucky guess," he said.

Rudy eyed Theo suspiciously.

The sun had set, and the dark of the evening set in quickly. In the valley below, a barrage of brightly colored fireworks exploded over the town of Mossville.

"You'd better get going," said Rudy.

"I can help you clean this stuff up," said Theo.

Rudy shook his head.

"No," he said. "Thank you. You've done enough for today. I'll take care of this stuff."

Theo nodded hesitantly, but his excitement for the festival was clear.

"You sure you're okay?"

"I'm fine!" said Rudy. "Now get out of here!"

Theo backed slowly across the field then broke into a run.

"Thanks, Dad!" he called out. He disappeared down the trail towards the valley.

Rudy watched Theo go. He appreciated his son's interest. Goodness knew he had done his best to encourage it, to the extent it was safe. There was no sense letting the boy into things he wasn't ready for. Theo often complained that Rudy was too protective; his rules were too strict. But Theo had no idea how lucky he was. It hadn't been this way for Rudy when he was a boy. His father Pythagoras Promovendis had been far less inclusive of Rudy in his work than Rudy was of Theo.

Sitting in the barley surrounded by the wreckage of his latest experiment, Rudy thought back to a day that had always remained vivid in his mind. It was close to 30 years ago now, not too long before the disaster had happened. He had been about the age Theo was now.

In his memory, Rudy leaped up and down in the thick mud, trying to peer into the dirty windows of his father's work shack. The shack had already sunk over a foot into the mud. Through the window, Rudy caught glimpses of large sheets of blueprints strewn across his father's workbench.

"Father!" Rudy called.

Pythagoras' face appeared for a moment in the window, then disappeared.

"Father!" Rudy shouted again.

The door of the shack opened a crack, pushing into the deep mud that embedded the shack. His father's lean, hawkish face peered through the crack, his eyes darting from side to side.

"Shh!" he hissed. "What is it, boy?"

"Can I help? Mother said you might let me help. I did all my chores!"

Pythagoras cast a glance up at the family house.

"Have you done the laundry?" he said.

"Yes!" said Rudy.

"Dishes?" Pythagoras asked.

"Yes!"

"What about the weeds, and the… the cleaning. Are the floors clean?" pressed Pythagoras.

"Yes!" Rudy said, an edge of desperation in his voice. "I did all that. Can I help?"

"No," said Pythagoras.

"But father!" cried Rudy.

"The less you know about my work, the better off you are."

"But I can help!" protested Rudy.

Pythagoras pushed his face into the crack in the door and fixed his son with a steely glare.

"Listen good," he said ominously. "There are all kinds of people in this world."

"So?" cried Rudy.

"So no," said Pythagoras. "Go help your mother."

With that, Pythagoras' face disappeared into the darkness and the door slammed shut. Rudy stared at the door as tears welled in his eyes.

Recalling the experience now, it was hard to keep the tears from welling up again. He had done his best to ensure that his own son would never feel that sting of exclusion. But lately he wondered whether it was for the best to let Theo so close to the dangers of his work.

Rudy collected the strewn contents of his pack and prepared to drag the huge machine back up the trail.

The machine was even heavier without Theo's help. Inch by inch, Rudy strained to pull it up the hill. He rested frequently under the darkening tunnel of trees that lined the road.

In the purple dusk, as fireworks popped in the distance, a swarm of bog aphids and gnats had re-convened over a corner of the field. Beneath the cloud of bugs lay the motionless crow.

The insects hung for several moments in the air, then descended in a tight funnel shape towards the dead black body of the bird. When the tip of the funnel reached the crow, the swarm rushed toward the crow at once and enveloped it. Aphids streamed into its mouth and gnats flew into and out of its nostrils.

The crow's body rocked slightly and its head appeared to twitch, nudged and tugged by the mass of tiny insects. A mass of aphids collected on its closed eye and pushed the eyelid open.

Suddenly, with a choking gasp, the crow gave a single violent flap of its wings. In a moment, the bugs dispersed and were gone.

Trudging up the path, Rudy heard the full-throated cry of a crow overhead. He looked up, but the black bird's shape was invisible among the evening trees.

Chapter 4
The Importance of Mayor Digniggleby

THE FESTIVITIES WERE JUST BEGINNING when Theo reached the center of Mossville. The town square was festooned with lanterns and ribbons and the crowd was thick. Theo had run all the way from the hills and by the time he got to the square he was so out of breath he could scarcely stand upright.

The square was a broad cobblestone plaza surrounded by faded baroque facades. In other times and other light, the facades had been pink and green and blue, but now they were only shades of the dusty violet sky. Narrow streets and even narrower alleys led from the square into the maze of the town center. Stone build-ings hundreds of years old jostled with newer wooden houses. In a quirk of Mossville architecture, the upper floors of the houses extended several feet beyond their ground floors, supported by heavy wooden struts, lending them an odd, unbalanced appear-ance. Red-tiled roofs were stacked one upon the next and a net-work of gutters and vines made it difficult to determine where one building ended and the next began. Wrought iron gas lamps—some affixed to lampposts and others ensconced on building walls—cast their flickering orange light over the crowd. People spilled out from the square into the snaking alleys and strained to see the festivities.

A stage was set up in the northeast corner of the square, where the ribbons that decorated the square came together in an extravaganza of bunting and bows. Over the stage hung a huge purple banner with the words MAYOR MERIWEATHER DIGNIGGLEBY: HERO OF MOSSVILLE written in sparkling gold lettering. On stage, a full brass band of schoolchildren performed a spirited selection of triumphant standards.

Behind the stage rose a dark shape that, at first glance, re-sembled nothing so much as a monstrous tree trunk. It was at least ten meters across and extended hundreds of meters into the sky. But the object was no tree. It was an enormous system of pipes, pumps, hoses and valves, all woven into a gigantic cylinder. The cylinder emerged from the cobbled ground of the square and soared up in a great arcing parabola that disappeared in the evening darkness. Its upper reaches were intermittently lit by fireworks. A deep, throbbing hum emanated from the structure and its shape pulsated in time with the hum.

It was no accident the stage had been positioned in front of this mechanical behemoth. This was the Suction-Flux Hydro-Debogilator, and it was thanks to it that the town of Mossville had anything to celebrate at all.

Theo squeezed through the audience, looking for a good place to watch the event. He was just a few yards from the stage, but the crowd was dense and the people were tall. Even when he jumped up and down, he could not get a glimpse of the activity on stage. A stout man shifted his weight and pushed Theo face-first into the broad bottom of a matronly woman who turned and swung her purse at Theo.

"Ragamuffin!" she shouted.

"Sorry!" cried Theo and ducked away.

Theo spied a ledge lined with flower boxes on the second story of a house not far from the stage. The corner of the ledge looked just big enough to sit on. A rusty gutter rose up the side of the house at an angle, and a patch of ivy clung to the wall near the ledge. Theo hopped onto the gutter and shimmied up. He scrambled across the ivy and began to hoist himself up onto the ledge, then he stopped.

Atop the ledge sat a brown toad about the size of Theo's fist. It sat smack in the spot where Theo had hoped to sit. It gazed at Theo with disinterest.

Theo strained to hold himself up. His belly leaned against the ledge, one foot was planted in the ivy, and one foot dangled freely without a foothold. He waved his head at the toad.

"Scoot!" he said.

The toad blinked, but did not move.

Theo sighed. He settled on his elbows. It wasn't comfortable, but at least he could see.

In front of the stage, the esteemed Constable Fleabo of the Mossville Municipal Police Department stood at attention with his team of policemen, a thin blue line to protect the evening's guests of honor from any rabble that might happen to become aroused. On the stage the guests of honor were assembled under the glare of spotlights. Mayor Meriweather Diniggleby, the man of the hour, stood center stage, glancing nervously from side to side. Mayor Diniggleby was a short, spherical man with no hair on his head save for two perplexed tufts for eyebrows and a cloud of ash-blond fuzz around his ears. He wore a white suit with a pink cummerbund that seemed to rise almost to his chin, leaving just enough room for a matching bow tie that was so tightly fixed to his ample neck it threatened to cut off his circulation. He wore a carnation in his lapel that matched the cummerbund, the tie, and indeed his very pink head itself. With apparent effort, he held his mouth in the shape of a broad smile, but his eyes made no such pretensions. Beside him stood his wife Cynthia and their twelve-year-old daughter Valerie. Cynthia Diniggleby was a tall, lean woman who towered over her husband and wore a look of perpetual disdain on her heavily made-up face. Her hair was done up in a perfectly rigid bouffant. Around her neck she wore a bushy, loosely knotted fox shawl, which still retained its head and paws as decoration. Her handbag, too, blurred the line between fashion and taxidermy, being composed of an intact cross-section an alligator's tail. The rest of her furs were mercifully free of identifying features, but it was clear that many minks had given their lives in the service of her apparel.

Valerie Diniggleby's style was less ostentatious than her mother's but no less meticulous. She wore a pink and beige polka-dotted dress with a matching beige petticoat. Her hat, purse and gloves were matching pink. Her hat was round with a narrow, upturned brim. The hat was decorated with cluster of roses and

33

bows—pink of course—and the blonde braids that fell over her shoulders were tied with matching ribbons. She stood upright with her feet together in beige patent leather shoes. She held an uncharacteristically worn doll firmly to her chest.

The expression on Valerie's face was something very near to angelic, the very picture of filial decorum. But from time to time, a momentary sharpness in her eyes as she glanced around the stage betrayed a restlessness that was altogether at odds with her overall demeanor.

A few feet behind and to the left of the family stood a tall, gaunt figure, half-lit by the spotlight. He was attired in a worn dark suit of indeterminable color and gripped the ball of a black cane, although his stiff, upright stance indicated he needed no support. His head and shoulders were only dimly visible beyond the penumbra of the spotlight. His deep-set eyes were visible only as two long, downward-pointing triangular shadows under a stern, overhanging brow. His head was wreathed in sparse, wiry gray hair. Even with his face in shadow he exuded an air of scorn.

Not many among the crowd would have recognized the figure to be Horace E. Cess, Chief Patent Administrator of the Mossville Municipal Office of Patent Registration and Processing. Fewer still would have thought to wonder why he shared the stage with the celebrated Digniggleby family. Those who did recognize Mr. Cess might well have wondered, but they would have had the good sense to keep their questions to themselves.

At the front of the stage, Mr. Cess' assistants Ballhatchet and Dooley stood before a tarnished, boxy microphone atop a short stand. Ballhatchet was a hulk of a man. He stood well over six and a half feet tall, with a wedge-shaped body that tapered downwards from his massive shoulders, upon which his disproportionately small head sat like an orange with a pompadour on a refrigerator. Dooley couldn't have been more than half the height of Ballhatchet. His body shape was nearly the precise opposite of Ballhatchet's. He resembled a dollop of whipped cream with his pointy head, spreading midsection, and short, widely-set legs. The two assistants wore matching black suits.

On the stage, Ballhatchet and Dooley seemed to be arguing about something. Dooley held a thick, stubby hand up over the microphone while trying to grab what looked like a crumpled piece of paper away from Ballhatchet, who held it just out of Dooley's reach. Dooley cast a glance in the direction of Mr. Cess, who nodded from the shadow. When the band children completed the rousing finale of their medley, Dooley stomped on Ballhatchet's foot and grabbed the paper. He nudged Ballhatchet roughly out of the spotlight and stepped forward to the mic.

Dooley tapped the mic and the sound boomed across the town square, followed by a squeal of feedback. He fumbled with the crumpled paper, cleared his throat loudly into the microphone, and began to read.

"Ladies and gentlemen, we are—" he began, then squinted at the paper with a puzzled expression. He shot an irritated sidelong glance at Ballhatchet, who mouthed a word to him. Dooley continued to read haltingly, "*gathered* here this evening to pay tribute to the hero of our time."

Dooley continued to read, looking over at Ballhatchet for support on every fifth word or so.

Theo's elbows hurt. The toad just stared at him.

"When Mossville faced its greatest crisis 20 years ago," read Dooley, "one man, endowed with a genius beyond the comprehension of ordinary people, rescued the city from a horrific fate. To Mayor Meriweather Diniggleby, for his brilliant invention of the Suction-Flux Hydro-Debogilator, we humbly extend our deepest, lasting gratitude."

As he said the name of the machine, he gestured at the towering structure behind the stage. The crowd applauded. Calls of "speech!" rose throughout the square.

Mayor Diniggleby stepped to the microphone, nodding uncomfortably at Dooley. He stood for a moment, blinking as though he had no idea how he had gotten there. He tried to clear his throat but hiccuped at the same time, resulting in a stifled, slightly painful sounding gagging noise. At last he spoke.

"I… uh," he began. "Thank you so much. You're entirely too kind. I'm very grateful for all of the, uh, gratitude."

A solemn hush enveloped the crowd.

"Indeed, what happened, or... nearly happened to our lovely town those years ago was... It was bad. Very, very bad. No doubt about it. It was, er, would have been, uh, very bad indeed. It could have been worse than it was, that is. Which is to say very bad. Indeed."

The crowd hung on every word. All eyes were on the Mayor.

"But the truth is..." he continued, then paused. His jowls trembled. Beads of sweat dotted his forehead.

If anyone had been watching Mr. Cess, they could not have failed to notice an almost electric jolt in his posture when he heard these words. His head snapped in the direction of the mayor like a bird of prey and he leaned in so stiffly and at such an angle that his body seemed almost to defy gravity. Digniggleby glanced towards Mr. Cess and winced.

"The truth *is* that the important thing is everybody's okay now and the bog is where it belongs, far away," he blurted.

The crowd cheered. The band struck up a vigorous march.

For reasons known only to itself, the toad on the ledge chose this moment to leap.

"Hey!" cried Theo.

The toad landed square on the top hat of a gentleman below. No sooner had the startled man looked up than the toad hopped again, this time directly into the crowded square.

Theo's stomach rose. The toad couldn't possibly last more than a few seconds in that crowd. Theo pictured the bad end it would surely come to on the cobbles of the square. He squeezed his eyes shut to banish the thought. With a rueful glance at the comfortable perch that would now go to waste, he swung himself down the ivy covered wall and dove into the crowd after the toad.

Now that he was no longer trying to watch the action up above, Theo could move quickly among the legs. He scurried in the direction of the toad's disappearance.

There it was, a motionless dark blob amid a sea of feet. The feet, however, were far from motionless. Boots, pumps, Oxfords and clogs hailed down from all directions around the toad. A booted foot came down smack on the spot where the frog sat and

Theo recoiled. He looked up to see the foot rise, with no sign of the toad underneath. A few yards away the movement of a dark blob landing on the ground caught Theo's eye. The toad had jumped away, miraculously unsmushed. Theo dashed after it, bumping legs and buckling knees as he went. He ignored the annoyed mutters and shouts that arose in his wake.

At last he caught up with the toad. He pushed past a fat man in a coat and tails who happened to be checking the time on his pocket watch. Theo dove after the toad. The toad jumped, but too late. Theo caught it in one hand and brought it close.

"Got you!" he said.

But Theo had gotten something else as well. Without his noticing, a stray thread from the sleeve of his worn sweater had caught itself on the chain of the fat man's pocket watch. When Theo had leaped after the toad, the watch had leaped after him.

"Thief! Pickpocket!" shouted the fat man. "Alert the authorities!"

For a moment, Theo had no idea the commotion had anything to do with him. He held the toad to his chest, cupped in both hands. He looked around to see what the fuss was about. The fat man was pointing straight at him.

"Stop him! Accost that rapscallion!" roared the fat man. Others began to take notice. A panic rippled through the crowd around Theo.

"A thief!" he heard someone say.

"Cover your goods!" said someone else.

"Let's get him!" said still another.

At once, the crowd seemed to descend upon him. In a panic, Theo ducked back down among the legs and scrambled away.

Theo had not realized how close he was to the stage, but now he burst through the front of the crowd to find himself face to face with the line of Mossville's finest. The commotion in the crowd had roused Constable Fleabo, whose head now whipped this way and that in an effort to identify the problem.

"Nothing to see here!" shouted Constable Fleabo reflexively. "Everything is under control!"

Theo dove back into the crowd.

The panic had reached the stage. Ballhatchet and Dooley stood back-to-back and assumed defensive Kung-Fu positions. The brass band descended into cacophony. Cynthia Digniggleby clapped her hands over Valerie's eyes.

"I want to see!" cried Valerie.

"You most certainly do not!" replied her mother. "You'll have nightmares for a week! Do something Meriweather!"

Mayor Digniggleby stood paralyzed with confusion.

"D-do…?" he babbled.

Constable Fleabo waded into the roiling crowd. A few moments later he reappeared, dragging Theo by the collar. Theo kicked and struggled helplessly.

"What do we have here?" asked Constable Fleabo.

"I didn't do anything!" cried Theo.

Valerie wrestled free of her mother and ran to the front of the stage, fascinated by the hubbub.

Theo and Valerie's eyes met. For just a fleeting instant, Theo thought he saw something in those eyes he could trust. He felt a flush of hope. He looked at Valerie imploringly.

As quickly as Theo's hope had appeared, it was gone. Valerie's face clouded as if she had caught herself doing something embarrassing. She stuck her tongue out and blew Theo a fat, wet raspberry.

Chapter 5
Business at the Patent Office

RUDY WORKED SILENTLY on the harvester. Theo sat nearby, holding the toad in front of his own face and frowning at it. From time to time Rudy extended his hand for some tool or other and Theo passed it to him. Theo always knew which tool Rudy needed without having to be told.

"It's always the same," Theo complained. "I get in trouble and it's not my fault."

Rudy stopped working, but didn't look up for several long seconds. Then he turned to Theo.

"Not your fault?" he asked. "The time you were caught with your pockets full of ball bearings wasn't your fault? The time they brought you in with a gyroscope stuffed down the front of your trousers wasn't your fault? Whose fault is it that you can't keep your hands from taking what you haven't paid for?"

Theo looked at his father with a pained expression.

"Why do you always take their side?" he asked. "It's bad enough that those stupid people think they're better than everyone."

Rudy winced.

"Don't you talk about Mayor Diggnigggleby that way!" he commanded.

"Why not?" said Theo. "That's what he is. He's like a big, fat clown. And Valerie Diggnigggleby, ew!"

Theo scrunched his face in disgust. "I don't know why everybody thinks he's so great."

Rudy thrust his face into Theo's angrily.

"Mayor Diggnigggleby saved this town. You don't know what it was like back then!"

Rudy knew he could never convey the disaster to his son. The youngster could know the facts, but he could never know what it was like to be there. What it was like to lose so much so suddenly.

"If it hadn't been for the mayor's work, more people would have died," he said. "Enough people died as it was!"

Rudy remembered the love and desperation on his mother's soot-black face when she burst through the flaming doorway at the moment he had seen her last. He remembered the horrible burbling of the mud as it consumed his father's work shed. Such violence, such abruptness. These weren't things Theo could ever understand. Truth be told, Rudy hoped Theo never would understand them. Theo had enough sadness of his own.

Rudy shook his head to clear out the memories.

"People love the mayor because of what he gave them. You ought to think about that."

Theo sat quietly, his eyes cast down. He glanced glumly at his toad.

The Mossville Municipal Office of Patent Registration and Processing was a wide, low building a few blocks away from the town square. The most notable thing about the patent office was the very large, very crooked house that seemed to float in the air about fifty feet above the main building. The house was supported by a cockeyed lattice of stilts and beams, up the center of which ran a wooden elevator shaft.

The house was wooden and weathered, and elegant in a way that a lunatic might have appreciated. It was a haphazard collection of balconies, gables, rooftops, and annexes tossed together in a towering, top-heavy heap. It had at least five or six stories, but its unconventional shape made it impossible to say how many exactly.

One long balcony looked out over the city. From another balcony extended a narrow, rickety maintenance catwalk that connected directly about a quarter of the way up the shaft of the Suction-Flux Hydro-Debogilator.

Just outside the door of one of the house's uppermost annexes stood a platform just big enough for one person to stand on at once. A small gondola composed of a vertical steel bar with a wooden bucket on the end was poised over the platform. From above the platform a system of gondola cables extended to a tall pole at the outskirts of Mossville and then further on to another pole well outside of the city. The cables extended further still into the haze in the direction of the ravine beyond the distant rocky ridge.

The house was the residence of Horace Cess, and the upper-most annex was his private office. He sat there now among the cabinets and bookshelves. Rolls of blueprints and plans formed a dense honeycomb in their racks against the wall. On the desk, paper and folders formed perfectly aligned but precariously high stacks. Next to the stacks sat a wood and metal intercom and a small copper and tin device, about the size of a pencil case, from which extended two metal arms. On each arm was a small reel, and between the two reels ran a narrow brown magnetic audio tape that wound through the device. From one side of the device extended a small, trumpet-shaped brass microphone.

A buzz sounded from the intercom. Mr. Cess pressed the button irritably.

"The mayor is here to see you," came the voice of Mr. Cess's secretary.

"Send him up!" said Mr. Cess. He reached across the desk and switched the recording device on. It clicked softly and the reels began to turn.

Mayor Digniggleby entered and took a seat. Mr. Cess sat behind his broad desk in an imposing high-backed leather chair. He idly organized the pencils on his desk, adjusting them repeatedly to be ever more parallel. The mayor sat in front of the desk in a small wooden chair that seemed ready to pop into splinters under his weight.

"I, for one, was not impressed," said Mr. Cess.

"E-excuse me?" said Mayor Digniggleby.

"Your so-called speech," said Mr. Cess. "You call that celebratory? You'd think twenty years as a hero to the masses would have endowed you with some rhetorical flair! I can only imagine what kind of noodle you'd be if you weren't universally adored!"

41

Mayor Diniggleby winced.

"I did try," he said.

Mr. Cess rolled his eyes.

"Regardless," he said.

"What we need to talk about is the baron."

"Oh dear," said Mayor Diniggleby. "Have you any idea how many sheep that man has?"

"I don't care how many sheep he has," said Mr. Cess. "We need the land. He must have tax issues."

"I don't know if I'm comfortable with this," said Mayor Diniggleby. "What do we need all that land for again, anyway?"

"Municipal projects!" Mr. Cess practically shrieked. "Do I have to spell everything out for you? What a question! As if one could ever have enough land!"

"Well, I—" began Mayor Diniggleby.

"Arrange a meeting with the Baron," interrupted Mr. Cess. "If I can't count on you, I don't know what the point is of any of this!"

"A-any of this?" repeated Mayor Diniggleby, his voice nearly a whisper.

Cess leaned forward over his desk and glowered down at Mayor Diniggleby.

"Twenty years is a long, long time to be hog-tied by the incompetence of another person," he hissed. "After all I've done for you!"

Mayor Diniggleby bit his lip. His jowls trembled.

"I-I understand Mr. Cess," he said. "I'll do my best."

Chapter 6
The Accidental Abduction of Baby Doll Bea

THE TOAD TOOK to Theo. The day after the celebration he had taken it out to Gurwell's field (which now sported a rather embarrassing haircut) and tried to let it go. But the toad did not go. It sat on the ground and stared at Theo. When he turned to go, the toad hopped after him.

"Are you going to follow me all the way home?" he asked. Of course, the toad did not answer, but follow him home is exactly what it did.

"Fine then," said Theo.

He named the toad Buford.

Over the next few days, it became clear that for someone whose work involved precisely controlling the behavior of hundreds of thousands of insects, a toad could be a troublesome pet. Theo's first attempt at getting back to his experiments was a disaster. Buford's lightning fast tongue   snapped up half a box of gnats before Theo even knew what was happening. It took Theo the better part of the next day out in the fields to replenish his supply.

Eventually, Theo built a special wooden pen on the windowsill for Buford. He concocted a mixture of cultured fungus and fly pheromone to lure a steady supply of bluebottles into the pen without affecting his own work. With Buford satisfied, Theo could get back to the business of creating his mechanical companion.

Theo's creation was making great progress indeed. It now had a full torso, two arms, and two legs, and the basis of a head. The body was a jury-rigged hodgepodge of spare parts and cast-off, tarnished widgets; it was no work of art, but it was functional. The head was a dense cluster of gears and clockwork movements that transformed into tangled, writhing explosion of insects and tethers when the bugs were activated.

Theo observed his creation. It lay across his desk, its shoulders and head propped up against the wall. Its extremities twitched and its body wriggled slightly as the bugs danced in and around it. They danced in clusters and streams, culminating in a swarming, orbiting mass around the head.

The automaton was working. But was it responsive?

Theo lunged forward and thrust his outstretched hands in the direction of the head. The whole body jerked as if by reflex, its arms stiffening symmetrically. His test was successful!

A smile crept across Theo's face. He'd done it! The parts were working together! It wouldn't be much longer now. From here on it was just a matter of adjusting chemical levels and refining the low-level training processes. After that, if Theo's assumptions were correct, emergent behavior should become automatic. His creation would take on a life of its own. The companion he'd imagined for so long would become real.

That head was a bit of a problem.

"You're going to have a hard time looking like that," he said glumly. "You'll scare everybody off."

Of course, the important thing was what was inside. But the outside was important too, thought Theo. His creation needed a face.

In the warm mid-morning sun, Cynthia and Valerie Digniggleby walked along the tidy cobblestones past the boutiques and pastry shops of Mossville's most exclusive shopping street. Cynthia wore a fuchsia and gold ensemble that involved feathers in a way that was not immediately clear to the casual observer. Valerie was dressed in a prim lavender and gray outfit with ankle-high gray suede lace-up boots. She held her worn cloth doll.

"What about a tiara?" said Cynthia. "Tiaras are nice for special occasions. A tasteful one. Just until you're old enough for earrings."

"I don't want a tiara," said Valerie.

"Well," said her mother petulantly. "You're not the one who buys your clothes, now, are you?"

"I'm the one who wears them," said Valerie.

Cynthia's eyes rolled upward then circled around to fall on Valerie's doll.

"And *that* old thing," she said, "has got to go!"

With that, she snatched Valerie's doll and tossed it in a nearby garbage can as they passed. Valerie's eyes went wide and her mouth fell open.

"We'll get you a better one!" said Cynthia.

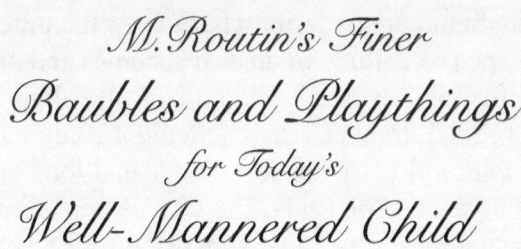

Cynthia took Valerie's hand before Valerie could say a word and led her into a shop whose front window was painted with a sign reading

M. Routin's Finer
Baubles and Playthings
for Today's
Well-Mannered Child

The two stood before a huge wall of baby dolls of all shapes and sizes. There were dolls made of cloth, wood, porcelain, plaster, and glass. They were dressed in all manner of clothing. Cynthia's eyes lit on a large doll with a graceful porcelain head and a bright yellow frilly dress. On the stand in front of the doll was a wooden plaque which read "BEA".

"Oh!" cried Cynthia.

"She's adorable!"

"What kind of a name is Bea?" said Valerie.

"It's a perfectly good name," said Cynthia. "Your father's aunt was named Beatrice."

"The seamstress?" said Valerie.

"Seamstress to royalty, sweetheart," corrected Cynthia.

"Dad never mentioned the royalty part," said Valerie.

"He's forgetful," said Cynthia.

Moments later the two emerged. Valerie held the doll and looked at it ambivalently.

"Well, the doll's an improvement, but look at you now!" said Cynthia. "The yellow doesn't go with your frock at all. Come along before too many people see you!"

Valerie looked over her shoulder at the garbage can. Her mother clutched her hand and pulled her down the street.

There was something for everyone in the bustling city center of Mossville. For Theo, trips to the city were an exciting glimpse at a world he was never quite part of. It was a tantalizing world full of action and camaraderie, where even the grocers and street vendors seemed to collude in unseen schemes and hijinks.

Rudy, for his part, had never taken the slightest interest in Mossville's social dramas. Any excitement Rudy had ever felt towards the commotion of the city center had long since dwindled to mere annoyance. For Rudy, the city center offered *parts*. And services, sometimes. But mostly parts. As he always did in the city, Rudy walked slowly, almost furtively, with a slight hunch. He glanced frequently from side to side. Crowds made him nervous.

Theo followed alongside, eagerly taking in the sights and sounds. He stopped in front of a wig shop and stared for a long moment at a bald mannequin head. He pursed his lips. It wasn't quite right. He ran to catch up with his father.

They arrived at a ramshackle wooden storefront with a hand painted sign reading FIONN'S HARDWARE. Below the name of the shop the words PARTS, CONSTRUCTION, SCREWS AND

NAILS, HOBBY SHOP, DIY, GASKETS & HOSE, and ONE-STOP were written. Halved wooden barrels and old crates filled with assorted metal widgets were stacked in front of the shop.

"Behave," said Rudy.

Theo looked hurt.

"What? I'm not gonna do anything bad!" he said.

Rudy paused a moment in front of the shop. He straightened up, sniffled purposefully, and walked into the store.

Fionn's Hardware store was dilapidated but very well stocked. Racks and boxes of parts and tools were stacked to the ceiling in all directions. Rudy approached the counter while Theo wandered into the maze of hardware, transported into a world of infinite possibilities.

The clerk was a sandy-haired man with overalls and a gray painters cap.

"Help you?" said the clerk.

Rudy mustered his social skills and answered as gracefully as he could.

"Sprockets," he said.

"Excuse me?" said the clerk.

"I'm looking for sprockets," said Rudy.

"Got those," said the clerk. "What do you need? Plate? Bossed? Simplex? Duplex? Shear pin? Bored to size? Mud relief? Idler?"

"Plate," said Rudy.

"Size?" asked the clerk.

"Two and a quarter inch," said Rudy.

"Sorry, plate sprockets don't come in two and a quarter. There's two and there's two and a half," said the clerk.

"Yes, they do," said Rudy.

Theo wandered the among the shelves and pallets of the shop. A pair of black rubber gloves caught his eye and he studied them approvingly. He found himself near the front window of the store.

Outside Valerie Digniggleby passed in front of the shop with her mother. Theo scowled to himself. It was better to just ignore people like them, he thought bitterly. He started to turn back to find his father.

Something in Valerie's arms caught his eye. It was a *face*, and in a split second Theo knew that it was just what he needed.

Valerie disappeared from the view of the cluttered hardware store window. Theo scrambled between two shelves to another window and caught sight of her again, but the yellow bundle in her arms was hidden by the crowd.

At the counter, Rudy was doing his best to remain courteous.

"I know what kind sprockets I need," he said.

"Well, sir," said the clerk, "I can only say that plate sprockets have not been manufactured in two and a quarter inch size since —"

But Rudy's response would not be contained.

"DO YOU HAVE ANY IDEA WHAT I AM BUILDING?!" he exploded. "DO YOU HAVE ANY IDEA WHAT A BOON IT WILL BE TO MOSSVILLE? TO MANKIND?!"

The clerk looked as though he had caught a small and highly localized pocket of windy weather directly in the face. He blinked a few times when the squall had passed.

"Sir, I am sure that I do not," he said.

"People!" scoffed Rudy and turned to leave.

He looked around the shop.

"Theo?" he said.

Stealth was not one of Theo's particular strengths. His hasty exit from the hardware store would surely have drawn his father's attention, if been so fully engaged in the sprocket conver-sation.

Theo trotted along the cobbles, keeping a few pedestrians be-tween himself and the mother and daughter pair as he tailed them down the street. He could hear snippets of their conversation.

"It's a perfectly lovely doll," said Cynthia.

"I liked my old one," sniffed Valerie.

Suddenly Valerie stopped.

48

"I need to tie my shoe," she said.

The pedestrians continued on their way around Valerie and her mother and Theo scrambled to find a place to hide. He ducked behind a narrow lamp post just a few feet behind Cynthia. As skinny as Theo was, the lamp post was much thinner, and he felt quite ridiculous trying to hide behind it. He prayed neither of the Dignigglebys happened to glance his way.

"Could you hold it?" said Valerie to her mother. Seeing her mother's dismayed expression she corrected herself. "Could you hold *her*?".

Cynthia took the doll as Valerie knelt in the middle of the sidewalk to tie the laces of her boot. At last Theo could get a good look at the doll.

It was perfect.

Not the doll itself, of course. The doll itself was just a stupid girl's toy. The dress, the little baby body, the stupid bonnet, those were useless to him. But the head. The head was perfect. It was just the right shape. Surely it was hollow and rigid enough to make adjustments to if necessary. The contours of the porcelain appealed to him. Maybe the red lips were a bit much, but other - wise, it was definitely something he could work with.

But how could he ever get Valerie to give it to him? He couldn't just walk up and ask for her new doll's head. He thought about it. Was there something he could offer to trade? That seemed unlikely. What did he have that someone like her could possibly want? The truth was, he didn't have much.

Buford wriggled in his pocket.

"Thanks for the offer, but I don't think Valerie Digniggleby wants a pet toad," said Theo softly.

But being traded off for the doll head was apparently not what Buford had in mind. He had simply decided, for reasons conceivable only to his own toad brain, that enough was enough of Theo's pocket. Before Theo knew what had happened, Buford leaped out of his pocket and directly onto Mrs. Digniggleby's chest.

What happened next seemed to unfold in slow motion for Theo. The time between the moment Mrs. Digniggleby felt a strange thump and the moment she was fully aware of a bumpy brown toad settled upon her bodice seemed much longer than just a second or two. When the realization finally hit, Mrs. Diggniggleby flung her hands up in the air and shrieked so loudly that all the shoppers within earshot froze.

The doll sailed into the air. Theo watched it arc towards the cobblestones. The porcelain head would be smashed to bits. Without thinking, Theo lunged for the doll and caught it only inches from the stones.

Mrs. Diggniggleby continued to scream and stomp and flail around well after Buford had hopped away. Valerie, still tying her shoe, looked over her shoulder to see what the commotion was all about.

Mrs. Diggniggleby's eyes fell on Theo, who was standing dumbly with the baby doll in his arms. All at once, she stopped her flailing.

"You!" she shouted.

Theo's eyes widened as he met Mrs. Diggniggleby's gaze. His mind raced. Valerie twisted herself awkwardly to see what was going on.

"THIEF!" shouted Mrs. Diggniggleby.

A dozen thoughts ran through Theo's mind at once. Valerie didn't want the doll anyway. She'd just *said* as much. It was only going to waste with these people. He, on the other hand, could put it to good use. He needed it. His creation needed it. Mrs. Diggniggleby was already calling him a thief, even though he'd done nothing wrong. She'd have him arrested either way if he let her. There was nothing to do but to run away, and he wasn't about to just drop the doll and let it shatter on the street. The passersby had begun to close in on him. He knew how it looked.

"Don't let him get away!" shouted Mrs. Diggniggleby.

There wasn't time to think it through any further. Theo cradled the doll in his arm and took off through the crowd. He disappeared around a corner into the maze of alleys just as Valerie finished tying her shoe.

Cynthia Diggniggleby's hysterics descended into incomprehensible blubbering as she commanded passersby to catch the thief and fetch the police. Valerie stood quietly with her hands on her hips, staring with steely anger in the direction Theo had run.

On a gray cobblestone, blissfully unaware of the commotion around it, sat Buford. He hopped once and disappeared around the corner after Theo. Valerie's eyes narrowed as she watched the toad go.

Chapter 7
The Questionable Accomplishments of
Mr. Horace E. Cess

THE MORNING WAS CRISP and bright as Rudy walked down the wooded path from the house to fetch the mail. It had been months since any mail had arrived, and months longer than that since Rudy had originally submitted the application for his patent. He knew the bureaucracy took time, but it was becoming difficult to hold out hope of ever receiving a reply.

So it was with great excitement that he found the officious looking letter in the mailbox with the return address stamped in authoritative capital letters: MOSSVILLE MUNICIPAL OFFICE OF PATENT REGISTRATION AND PROCESSING. A gleeful squeal emerged from Rudy's throat and he instinctively glanced around to see if anybody had heard him. He had to fight just to keep from jumping in the air and clicking his heels. He bounced slightly as he tore the envelope open and unfolded the contents.

It was his original patent application. Running diagonally across the page in huge red letters, the word REJECTED was stamped. He stopped bouncing.

Folded behind the application was a letter. The letter read:

> Dear Inventor,
>
> We regret to inform you that your patent application has been rejected.
>
> Best Regards,
>
> Horace E. Cess
> Chief Patent Administrator
> MMOPRP

Tears welled up in Rudy's eyes. He stood on the path for a long time.

The main office area of the Mossville patent office consisted of a single, sprawling, windowless room. Most of the surfaces had been painted pale slate gray many years previously in order to minimize distractions for the workers, and the paint job showed its age. Rows and rows of modest wooden desks stretched to the back of the room, each equipped with a type-writer, a wooden rack of rubber stamps, a deep wooden in-box at the left corner, and a deep, wooden out-box at the right corner. At each desk a gray-clad patent office employee worked diligently on his or her paperwork. The uniform of patent office workers consisted of a light gray shirt, dark gray slacks and tie for men and dark gray skirt and sailor scarf for women.

In the center of the room stood an elevator. The elevator had clearly been constructed as an afterthought, added to the original building with little if any planning. Iron pulleys, cables, gears and flywheels stood exposed, looking entirely out of place—and more than a little hazardous—against the austere background of the room.

At the front and center of the room, between the rows of desks and the public entrance, stood another desk with a placard that read RECEPTION. On this desk sat a rusty intercom. A uni-formed office lady sat behind this desk.

To the left of the public entrance, facing the reception desk, stood a long row of wooden chairs. Rudy sat in one of these chairs. Other somewhat unkempt middle-aged men sat to either side of him. All of them, including Rudy, looked nervous and ill-at-ease.

A man's voice came through the intercom, barking a curt or-der. From where Rudy sat there was far too much distortion to make out exactly what the voice said. The receptionist responded quietly into the intercom, then raised her head.

"Promovendis," she said.

"Yes, that's me," said Rudy.

"The Chief Patent Administrator will see you now," she said.

The elevator doors behind the receptionist opened. She gestured for Rudy to enter.

"You're awfully fortunate, Mr. Promovendis," she said as he passed her desk. "Mr. Cess rarely meets personally with claimants."

The elevator ride was as rickety and harrowing on the inside as the elevator looked on the outside. Rudy stepped out of the elevator considerably more rattled than he had been going in. He found himself in the middle of a cluttered, dimly-lit office.

Seated in a high-backed leather chair behind a large desk was the Chief Patent Administrator.

"Don't trouble yourself to sit down," said Mr. Cess. "This shouldn't take long. What can I do for you?"

Rudy reached timidly across the desk and handed his rejected application to Mr. Cess.

"I... this... I think there must be some mistake," he stammered.

Cess glanced at the application, then tossed it on the desk.

"I see," he said.

"I need the patent to protect my work," said Rudy.

Mr. Cess pressed his fingertips together and looked upward, as though pondering how best to explain a difficult concept.

"Well, you see, I'm afraid that's the problem," he said. "Patents can only be granted to original works."

"B-but," protested Rudy, "the invention is unprecedented! And the mechanisms can be generalized to create an endless variety of devices. I'm going to change the world with these technologies! How could anybody think this is not worthy of a patent?"

Mr. Cess looked Rudy in the eye.

"Oh, it is worthy of a patent," he said. He reached down and withdrew a rolled up set of plans from a pile of similar rolls behind his desk. He slowly unrolled the plans and spread them out across the desk.

"Unfortunately, someone seems to have beaten you to it," he said.

There, diagrammed in precise detail, complete with measurements and annotations, was Rudy's harvester. The handwriting was his, the drawings were the very ones he had labored over for years. Every component, every mechanism, every brilliant idea he had had over the course of the past two decades was there in those plans.

Across the top of the page, the words "Promovendis Insect-Powered Hillside Harvester" could still be made out. But the name on the plans had been awkwardly altered with what looked like tempera paint to read "CESS".

The plans were stamped with large green stamps reading *AP-PROVED*.

"I don't understand," gasped Rudy. "That's my... How... Who?"

"I suppose great minds think alike," said Cess.

Rudy stood motionless, confused and shocked beyond words.

"I'd be very interested to know who, aside from yourself, has been party to this unfortunate miscommunication," said Cess.

Rudy blinked uncomprehendingly, mouthing Cess's words to himself to try and make them make sense.

"Who else knows about the machine?" asked Cess.

"Who else knows?" said Rudy in a daze. "Why, nobody. Just me and my s—"

Rudy stopped himself, but it was too late. A terrible understanding began to creep over him. This was no miscommunication.

Cess leaned forward.

"Your son?" he said.

"Now hold on," said Rudy. "You leave my son out of this. He is not involved in my work in any way."

Cess smiled agreeably. "Of course not."

Rudy looked around the office. On the desk the reels of the patent administrator's pocket-sized reel-to-reel recording device turned quietly.

"I don't know what's going on here," he said. "But if you're trying to steal my invention, you won't get away with it!"

Cess stood.

"My dear man," he said. "There's no need for talk like that. Here, come this way. I have something to show you that I think will render this little dispute quite beside the point."

"Show me?" said Rudy.

Cess walked to a wood door at the side of his study and opened it. It opened out onto a small platform from which a rather magnificent view of Mossville city center could be seen. At the far edge of the platform was a vertical steel pole which rose beyond the view of the door. On the pole hung a wooden sign shaped like the outline of a hand with the index finger extended pointing away from the city. The sign read KOOK BOG.

"Step this way please," said Cess, gesturing towards the balcony.

Still shocked and confused, and now increasingly curious, Rudy stepped out onto the platform. He looked out over the breathtaking scene.

Cess pressed a large red button on the wall. The label of the button read KOOK BOG GONDOLA LAUNCH.

Suddenly, the Kook Bog Gondola roared to life. Rudy looked up to see the bullwheel at the top of the pole start to turn and the overhead cables jerk into motion. It took him just a moment to understand the significance of these movements, but it was a moment too long.

The gondola itself was an angled wooden bucket at the end of a metal pole. It swung down to the platform and scooped Rudy up in a flash, catching him by the rear end and wedging him in tightly as it sailed upward along its cable and away into the misty yonder.

Rudy's screams faded into the distance. Cess watched him go with an expression of grim satisfaction.

Many years previously, a very young Horace Cess had decided what he wanted to be when he grew up. At the time, he lived in a large orphanage in the outskirts of Greater Mossville

County. He had lived there as far back as he could remember, ever since—he had been told—his parents had been killed by an alligator while picnicking. If not for his father's slide-rule becoming stuck in the beast's craw, Baby Horace too would surely have perished.

Cess remembered as if it were yesterday the evening his ten-year-old self sat at the long table in the orphanage mess hall staring at the steam rising up from his soup.

The orphan beside him, a boy named Geaner, looked at him quizzically.

"Why are you staring at your soup?" said Geaner.

"I'm studying to be a scientist," said young Cess.

"You can't be a scientist," said Geaner.

"Yes I can!" said Cess angrily. "I'm going to have a booth in the Mossville Young Scientist Fair! And I'm going to win the prize!"

Geaner just looked at Cess's soup.

"I don't see what's scientific about soup," he shrugged.

But young Cess had not been dissuaded. Night after night, he waited in his bunk as the lights went out in the dormitory of the orphanage, staring at the warped plywood of the bunk above him. Through the windows of the dormitory he could see the lights go out in other parts of the building. He waited until he was sure everybody in the orphanage was fast asleep.

He took a small, tattered notebook, a stump of pencil, and a tarnished copper pocket watch from under his pillow. Along with the slide-rule, a ladies' boot heel, and a piece of belt, the watch had been all that had remained of his parents after their fateful marshland picnic.

Young Cess sneaked past the bunks of sleeping orphans and out of the dormitory. He made his way through the darkened halls of the orphanage until he reached the vast kitchen that served all of the orphanage's over five hundred young residents.

Every night, he went straight to the same corner of the kitchen, where the moon and a dim night lamp outside the window cast enough light for him to work. He rummaged through a large metal drawer to find a baking thermometer and a pan.

He filled the pan with cold water from the tap, placed it on the stove, and lit the hob. He placed the thermometer into the water, set the watch on the counter, and began to take notes. By the time the water boiled, he had filled a page with scribbled notes. He dumped the pan out in the sink, filled it up again, adjusted the flame on the hob, and repeated the process again and again and again.

His research continued in this manner for weeks. For all that time, he managed to conceal his activities from the adults of the orphanage. He feigned illness to explain his lack of sleep. Participation in activities outside the orphanage was discouraged in order to prevent orphans from joining the circus or embarking on a life of crime. But even if he had managed to beg and bargain for permission to participate in the science fair, it was strictly forbidden for orphans to enter the kitchen under any circumstances. He would have had nothing to present.

At last, the day of the Mossville Young Scientist Science Fair arrived. Young Cess had constructed an elaborate excuse to leave the orphanage for the day. His usual Saturday physical education instructor thought he was helping the orphanage librarian stack boxes of old books. The librarian thought he was running errands for the headmaster of the orphanage. The headmaster thought he had been requisitioned by the cook to make a trip to the market. The cook knew nothing of any of this and wouldn't have recognized Young Cess anyway.

There were at least fifty booths set up in the town square and an impressive crowd had gathered of parents and relatives of the young scientists.

Young Cess set up his booth by himself. It had not been easy to make his poster. He had cut the paper to size by hand without scissors (which were forbidden in the dormitory area) and had drawn the poster with his pencil stub and bits of crayon he had stolen from the orphanage's art room. All of this, furthermore, he had done in the dark. He had done his best, but the results were far from what anyone could call polished.

The poster featured a series of drawings of pots and water, each accompanied by a column of neatly hand-written times and temperatures. Across the top of his poster the title was written in green crayon: HOW WATER BOILS with the word FAST written in pencil above the rest and squeezed in as an afterthought with a lit-tle arrow between the words "how" and "water". Young Cess had felt that the original title had implied a more thorough explanation of the phenomenon than his measurements could really provide. Standing before his poster now he felt a tinge of regret for his ex-cessive modesty.

The other exhibits were far more sophisticated. To Cess's right a tidy, bespectacled lad stood before a presentation titled "The Mating Rituals of the Bonobos". The booth was adorned with expertly-drawn pictures, stunning photographs, and tidy, typewritten notes. The centerpiece of the presentation was a re-markably lifelike clockwork diorama featuring two hand-carved wooden bonobos circling each other and performing what looked like dance moves.

To Cess's right, a blonde girl in curls presided over an exhibit titled "The Physics of Aviation", which featured beautifully de-signed poster, a fully-functional miniature wind tunnel, and a small armada of tiny working balsa-wood flying machines that circled in the air around the presenter.

Other exhibits included a clockwork model of the solar sys-tem complete with moons, a model locomotive that used electro-magnets to levitate over its tracks, and a life-sized skeletal replica of the missing link between humans and apes.

Family members and loved ones thronged around the booths, oohing and aahing over the projects. They moved quickly past Cess's booth, avoiding eye contact.

"So sad," he heard a lady say as she passed by. "I don't think they should let them enter. It will only make them feel bad."

"He's probably the only one here who actually made his own project," said the man she was with.

"Still, look at it," said the lady. "Poor thing."

Cess stood by his poster for the duration of the fair, fighting back tears as he looked at the other booths and their visitors.

As the crowd began to thin later in the day, a rumpled, mid-dle-aged man approached Cess's booth. When he looked at Cess directly, Cess stood at attention. Cess had spent days preparing his little talk, and was excited to finally have a receptive audience.

"I couldn't help but notice your notes," said the man.

"Really?" said Cess.

"I think you have a talent, my boy," said the man.

Cess was dumbstruck. He couldn't remember having ever received a compliment of such a magnitude.

"A-a talent?" he said. "Really?"

The rumpled man nodded.

"My name is Lobodin," said the man. "I am the headmaster of a clerical school for orphans. I think you would be an excellent candidate for enrollment."

Cess's excitement disappeared.

"Clerical?" he said.

"Your notes are very thorough," smiled Lobodin. "I think you would make an excellent clerk."

Cess's face darkened.

"I'm not a clerk," he said. "I'm a scientist."

Lobodin looked at Cess's poster. He raised his eyebrows in an expression Cess could not help but interpret as pity.

"No!" shouted Cess. "I'm a scientist! Go away!"

Lobodin shrugged. He took a calling card from a small leather case and slipped it into Cess's shirt pocket.

"If you change your mind," he said. Then, with a friendly smile he turned to leave.

"I'm not going to change my mind!" Cess called after him. "I'm no clerk!"

Cess took the card from his pocket and threw it savagely onto the ground.

"Clerk!" he shouted again. His voice cracked and he stifled a sob.

Young Cess's booth had been the last one standing that day. He stood there until long after the other young scientists and their parents had dismantled theirs. When he returned to the orphanage he learned that the physical education instructor, the librarian, the headmaster, and the cook happened to belong to the same Saturday afternoon Pinochle club and his absence had been discovered. He was severely reprimanded and lost privileges for a month, but he no longer cared. His dreams had been dashed.

Mr. Cess had never fully understood what had made him pick Lobodin's card up from the ground and take it with him back to the orphanage. But it had been a fateful decision. That card had put him on the path that would one day lead him here, all these years later, to this platform high above the town of Mossville.

He watched the gondola disappear into the misty yonder amid the fading echoes of Rudy Promovendis' screams.

"Clerk, indeed," he sneered to himself.

He stepped back into his office and closed the door.

Buford the toad was sitting expectantly in his pen on the win-dowsill when Theo woke late after a night of furtive work on his creation. The little hopper for the fungus and fly pheromone was empty. Theo filled it up and left Buford to his breakfast.

Rudy was not at home. There was nothing unusual about this in the Promovendis house; for the most part, father and son came and went as they pleased. Time alone in the house was time Theo could devote more freely to his project. Especially today, when cutting and drilling the ceramic head to fit the machinery was likely to be a noisy process, having the run of the place was a welcome surprise.

It was not by chance that Rudy's workshop was positioned to afford a clear view down the front path of the house. It was one of ways in which Rudy's own paranoia often aided Theo in keeping his activities hidden from his father. Theo kept one eye on the path as he set to work on the head.

Theo sheared off the crown of the porcelain head. This would give the head mechanism enough room to operate and allow free movement of the bugs. He drilled holes in the base of the head for the screws to affix the head to the neck. He cut a few more small panels from the back of the head to enable access for repairs and adjustments. The process took about an hour. He was cleaning porcelain powder from the work area when movement caught his eye outside the window.

He ducked down instinctively. Through the open window he could hear the voices of two men and their heavy footsteps coming up the path. He poked his head up cautiously to sneak a look.

Constable Fleabo and another officer were approaching the house.

They didn't look happy.

Chapter 8
The Suction-Flux Hydro-Debogilator and the Unsung Savior of Mossville

THE HOME OF BARON LLEWELLYN LePeen was a stately manor built in the neoclassical style and painted a dusty rose color that the baron was extremely fond of. The inside of the manor was ornate and reflected the baron's refined taste. The salon where the baron now sat with Mayor Digniggleby and Mr. Cess was predominantly the same dusty rose color of the outside of the building. The room was adorned with gorgeous neoclassical panels of deep purple venetian plaster on the wall and a *trompe l'oeil* fresco on the ceiling featuring several dozen fat, winged cherubs who appeared to float upward over the room towards an overflowing pot of gold that hovered—literally at the end of a rainbow—in the sky above. was deep reddish walnut with brass fixtures.

Mayor Digniggleby and Mr. Cess sat on chairs with maroon velvet cushions while the baron reclined across a small table from them in his stocking feet atop a matching chaise longue.

"So, you want to buy my land," said the baron.

Mayor Digniggleby nodded.

"Yes, that's right," he said.

The baron waved a finger in the air.

"Bartholomew!" he called.

A butler appeared immediately, as if out of nowhere.

"Two glasses of wine please," said the baron. He glanced at Mr. Cess, who sat hunched and glowering in his drab, charcoal-colored suit. "And a cup of coffee for the clerk."

Cess stiffened. The baron smiled widely at him.

"We need you to be attentive to the details, after all!" said the baron jovially.

The baron now turned back to Mayor Digniggleby.

"So then. You see, the thing is," he said, "I have a great many sheep."

He turned to Cess.

"Four hundred and sixty-two," he enunciated.

Mr. Cess's pocket sized reel-to-reel recording device turned quietly on the table between them.

"Indeed," said Mayor Digniggleby.

"So I don't think I'm interested," said the baron.

"I see," said Mayor Digniggleby.

Mr. Cess leaned over and whispered into Mayor Digniggleby's ear. Mayor Digniggleby's forehead wrinkled worriedly and his jowls trembled.

"Uhh," said Mayor Digniggleby.

Bartholomew appeared with two glasses of wine and a cup of coffee on a silver tray. He placed the wine in front of the baron and Mayor Digniggleby and the coffee in front of Cess. Cess looked disdainfully at the coffee. The baron raised his wine glass to Mayor Digniggleby, who reluctantly raised his own in response.

"Cheers!" said the baron.

Mayor Digniggleby downed his wine in a gulp.

"So I suppose we're finished here then!" said the Baron. He turned to Cess. "Please send a transcript of your notes to my secretary by the end of the work week. I'm sure I can count on you to be thorough!"

"Well," said Mayor Digniggleby timidly.

"Yes?" said the baron.

"There was one other thing I had, uh, hoped to bring up," said Mayor Digniggleby. He looked around. "But I suppose maybe I—"

He cleared his throat. Then he coughed. His eyes watered.

The baron raised his eyebrows.

"Never mind," said Mayor Digniggleby, wincing visibly under Cess's furious glare.

Mr. Cess was still fuming as they left the baron's manor.

"I just couldn't threaten him," said Digniggleby. "After his hospitality and whatnot."

Cess said nothing.

"Sorry about the coffee," said Mayor Digniggleby.

Cess stared straight ahead.

It was like a curse, thought Cess. To have so much power within his grasp and yet all at the mercy of this incompetent buffoon. It was the only drawback of what had once been such a perfect plan, but what a ruinous drawback it was.

Cess remembered the day it had all begun. It was in the midst of Mossville's darkest times; the catastrophe was in an advanced stage and advancing mercilessly with each passing day. People went about their daily business, some feigning ignorance, some mutely ignoring the encroaching horror as if willing the reality to become unreal. But everyone knew the truth deep down. Mossville was helpless, sinking like a drowning rat.

The patent office was much the same then. Except, of course, there was no elevator, nor any place above for an elevator to go.

In those days, Cess was a young man. He had never been an especially robust person, but he stood without hunching and he still had most of his brown hair, thinning though it may have been.

Cess's desk was just one among the sea of desks in the patent office. He was responsible for receiving applications. Day after day he took applications, engaged applicants in a brief interview, and sent the paperwork on its way.

"You should be hearing from our office within the next eight to twenty-four weeks," he said hundreds of times a day. "Please do not contact our office until you have received notice."

The clerk to Cess's left was named Barlow. Barlow was a bit unkempt and prone to mistakes, but friendly and good-natured.

An applicant left Barlow's desk and Barlow turned to Cess.

"There's an idea that'll make him rich," said Barlow. "Powdered whiskey."

Cess glanced at Barlow. He didn't mind Barlow. Sure, Barlow was basically a waste of space who would never accomplish anything of any importance and was doomed to toil away in soul-crushing tedium just like all the rest of the clerks. But as wastes-of-space went, Barlow was bearable, and occasionally even showed hints of spunk.

"Y'know," said Barlow more quietly. "Sometimes I think it sure would be tempting to just, y'know, take one of these ideas. I mean, there are so many of them! Who'd be the wiser? But then, I suppose straight arrows like Felix run such a tight ship around here that none of us could get away with something like that."

Barlow gestured idly at the desk across the room where the neatly-combed, bespectacled Felix sat, diligently organizing papers and checking stamps and signatures. Felix's desk was impeccably tidy.

"I suppose not," said Cess. He paused a moment before returning to his work. "Next!"

It had been that very day that Pythagoras Promovendis had taken his seat across from Cess's desk and presented his application.

Pythagoras was even more furtive and cagey than the average patent-seeker. His eyes darted back and forth as he passed the stack of forms and plans across the cluttered desktop. Written in the "Invention Name" field of the main application form were the words "Suction-Flux Hydro-Debogilator." Cess looked over the form and skimmed the plans.

"What does it do?" he said.

"It will reverse the advance of the bog," said Pythagoras.

Cess pricked up his ears. The fingers of his left hand unconsciously scratched at he caked mud that covered his pant legs nearly up to the knees. It was the same mud that covered everyone's trousers in Mossville. He wondered for a moment how it could have been so easy for so many people to grow accustomed to trudging through three feet of mud wherever they went.

"Reverse?" said Cess.

"It will save this city," said Pythagoras.

"That would certainly be something," said Cess.

"Yes," said Pythagoras.

Cess looked over the submission form more closely. Everything seemed to be in place. He slid the form towards Pythagoras and pointed to the space for the inventor's signature.

"I need you to sign here," he said.

Pythagoras moved forward to sign. Suddenly, the entire room tilted sickeningly. Items tumbled from the shelves and clerks gripped their desks. Shifts like these had become a daily feature of life in Mossville lately.

Pythagoras fixed Cess with wide, wild eyes.

"There is no time to waste!" he said.

"Indeed!" said a shaken Cess.

Pythagoras signed his name rapidly, still staring at Cess, as if to further impress upon him the importance of the application.

"You should be hearing from our office in the next," Cess's voice trailed off, "eight to twenty-four weeks."

"This town should be so lucky to still be standing then," hissed Pythagoras.

Cess nodded.

"I'll do what I can," he said.

Cess sat quietly for a moment after Pythagoras had left. He knew it was true. The invention was Mossville's only hope, at a time when hope was exactly what the city needed.

Cess set the Promovendis application in his out-box. He was about to call the next applicant when he noticed something. The inventor's signature was not on the application.

Puzzled, Cess ruffled through the papers on his desk to see if somehow he had gotten two copies of the application form. He quickly found the culprit: a blank sheet of typing paper, across the top edge of which was the freshly scrawled signature of Pythagoras Promovendis. The sheet of paper must have slid across the form when the ground had shifted. Without noticing, Pythagoras had signed his name to the wrong paper.

Instinctively, Cess rose from his chair and made to chase after Pythagoras. Surely he could catch him before he had gotten far. The little mix-up could be quickly rectified.

But then he stopped.

Perhaps, he thought to himself, now was not the time to do anything hasty. He sat back down slowly. He looked again at the unsigned form, then tucked it into his desk drawer.

There were other applicants waiting.

"Next!" he said.

Later that evening, Cess sat in his desk doing paperwork as his colleagues left the office one by one.

Felix passed his desk.

"Don't overtax yourself!" said Felix.

Cess smiled vaguely.

"Just a few things I need to finish up," he said.

When the last clerk had left Cess sat alone in the light of his desk lamp. He took the Promovendis application out of the desk and stared at it for a long time.

Chapter 9
The Inventing of an Inventor

THE NEXT DAY CESS was unusually attentive as he conducted his interviews. In addition to the standard patent office questions he asked every day, he threw in a few of his own. He studied the applicants' facial expressions and carefully noted their responses to his comments and questions. He wasn't entirely sure what he was looking for, but he felt confident he would know it when he saw it.

A pudgy, blank-faced young man sat across from him. He looked like a lump of bread dough with red cheeks.

"Name?" said Cess.

"Diniggleby," said the man. "Meriweather."

"Application form and plans," said Cess.

Diniggleby passed a single sheet of paper across the table.

"I wasn't too sure about how to fill out the form," he said. "But here are the plans."

Cess looked at the plans. There was nothing on the paper but a drawing of an oval.

"This?" said Cess.

Diniggleby nodded enthusiastically.

"What is it?" said Cess.

"It's a paperweight!" said Diniggleby.

"A paperweight," said Cess.

Diniggleby nodded again.

"You do realize an invention has to be new in some way to be eligible for a patent," said Cess.

"Oh, but it is!" said Diniggleby. "See, it's oblong! And it's made of soap!"

"Oblong?" said Cess.

"To fit in your hand better! It's much easier to pick up than a round paperweight!" said Diniggleby. "At least, in theory."

Sensing that Cess was not impressed, Diniggleby continued with even greater urgency.

"A-and when your hands get dirty from handling all the inky paper, it doubles as soap!" he said.

Cess looked at Digniggleby for a long moment without speaking.

"I see," he said at last.

Digniggleby smiled blankly.

"May I ask you a question?" said Cess.

"Sure," said Digniggleby.

"How would you like to own the patent for something important?" said Cess. "For something that will make you, overnight, the most beloved man in this town?"

"The paperweight?" said Digniggleby.

"No," said Cess.

"Well," said Digniggleby, "I don't know... I haven't really invented anything else."

"That's not what I'm asking," said Cess. "I'm asking if you would like to own the patent."

Digniggleby looked puzzled.

"You see," explained Cess, "it seems we have some unclaimed patents lying around, and I have been asked to find worthy owners for them. I think you fit the bill."

"Really, I do?" said Digniggleby.

Cess smiled.

"Yes," he said. "You really do."

And so began the salvation of Mossville.

After Cess fast-tracked the patent application, things moved very quickly. The town's denial of the catastrophe vanished when they realized a solution had been found, and the citizens quickly rallied to build the Suction-Flux Hydro-Debogilator. It was far and away the most ambitious construction project that had ever broken ground anywhere in the vicinity of Greater Mossville County. Cess and Digniggleby stayed on site throughout the process. They made an odd pair in their hard hats and protective boots. Cess barked orders to construction workers while Digniggleby smiled agreeably and watched in bewilderment as the plans unfolded around him. The massive arch of pipes and pumps ex-

70

tended high into the sky, its far end disappearing into the ravine beyond the distant ridge.

When the construction was finished, Digniggleby, with an embarrassed grin and an ill-fitting suit, cut the ribbon. Cess stood behind him to one side. The huge machine groaned and rumbled to life. Hoses and tubes that rose along its shaft began to pulsate and the throbbing hum of its pumps made the ground beneath the town square tremble.

Throughout Mossville, the mud began to recede and the ground began to dry and harden. Soon it was clear to everyone that the catastrophe had been averted. Digniggleby's Suction-Flux Hydro-Debogilator had saved the town.

Hailed as a hero, Digniggleby's personal advancement was swift. After a week of celebration, he was awarded the keys to the Mayor's mansion for life. No-one had ever done so much for Mossville, felt the citizens. If it had not been for Meriweather Digniggleby and his extraordinary invention, the entire city would have perished. It was the least they could do in gratitude.

With a friend in such a high place, Mr. Cess's fortunes soon changed for the better as well. By Mayoral Decree, Cess was promoted to Chief Patent Administrator. Municipal funding was allocated to ensure he had the resources necessary to carry out his duties effectively. After all, it was thanks to his rapid processing of Digniggleby's patent that the town had been saved.

The necessary resources turned out to include a luxurious elevated personal residence built to Mr Cess's exact specifications directly over the patent office, accessible via private elevator. Among his specifications were plans for a cable gondola that extended from a platform on his home into the distant ravine beyond the ridge.

Far away, in that deep, misty ravine beyond the ridge, the other end of the Suction-Flux Hydro-Debogilator was embedded in the ground. Wet mud burbled around it.

Twenty-four weeks and one day after the submission of his patent application, Pythagoras Promovendis sat angrily in the waiting area of the patent office.

"The Chief Patent Administrator will see you now," said the receptionist, gesturing towards the elevator. "Right this way."

As Pythagoras passed her desk she remarked, "You're very fortunate. Mr. Cess rarely meets with claimants."

The intervening years had not been especially kind to Felix the clerk. His organizational skills were as sharp as ever, but a hollowness had crept into his eyes. His face had become gray and thin along with his perfectly-combed hair. He stood now before Mr. Cess's desk.

"You know how I feel about numbers, Felix," said Cess. "It's why you're down there and I'm up here."

Felix nodded.

"Yes, of course," he said. "But I really feel these inconsistencies require your attention."

Cess rolled his eyes.

"Fine. What do you want to tell me?" he said.

"It's the records from human services, sir," said Felix.

"Yes," said Cess.

"Well, sir, it's considered standard for personnel to receive a pay raise every two years to account for costs of living," said Felix.

"And?" said Cess.

"Well, sir, it has been quite some time since the clerical department has received a raise," said Felix. "To be precise, we haven't received a raise since..."

Felix trailed off.

"Since?" prompted Cess.

"Well, sir, since you took over as Chief Patent Administrator twenty years ago," said Felix.

"I see," said Cess.

"I thought you should be aware of that," said Felix.

Cess sat quietly for a long moment, fingertips pressed together. His eyes narrowed.

"The next time you feel the urge to bring this kind of clerk trivia to my attention," he said, "I hope you have a more compelling reason than your own personal greed. You ground-floor paper pushers are paid every penny of what you're worth. The day you become worth more is the day you'll get a raise. Which, frankly, is not a day I see coming any time soon."

Felix opened his mouth to protest, but stopped, not knowing quite what to say.

"Speaking of pay, don't you have some kind of work you ought to be doing to earn yours?" said Cess.

In the city center of Mossville, Ballhatchet and Dooley were posting fliers. Ballhatchet nailed one to a wooden post. It read:

PUBLIC ANNOUNCEMENT OF
AN EXTRAORDINARY NEW INVENTION
TOMORROW 2:00 *SHARP*
MOSSVILLE TOWN SQUARE

"I'm excited about this," said Ballhatchet.

"You don't even know what the invention is," said Dooley.

"I bet it's baby wigs!" said Ballhatchet.

"Baby wigs?" said Dooley.

"Every time I see a baby, I think, why doesn't he have hair? It doesn't make sense for babies to be bald like that," said Ballhatchet.

Dooley sneered.

"I doubt Mr. Cess is planning to announce baby wigs, Ballhatchet," he said.

73

"No need to be so negative," said Ballhatchet.

Dooley shook his head and nailed a flier to a wooden cobbler shop sign.

"Hey!" cried the proprietor from inside the shop.

"Municipal authorities," said Dooley. "Back off."

Chapter 10
An Overwhelming Display

CONSTABLE FLEABO AND DEPUTY DEEPAK of the Mossville Police Department stood at the front door.

"Promovendis!" barked Constable Fleabo. "Police! We've got a warrant to search these premises! If you don't grant us admission to this house by your own voluntary free will we will be compelled to break down this door!"

"Maybe we should try the door first," said Deputy Deepak.

"No need to be hasty, deputy," said Constable Fleabo.

He shouted again the door.

"Promovendis!" he said. "This is the police! Your failure to grant us admission will leave us with no alternative but to forcefully enter these premises! I am legally obligated to inform you furthermore that any and all costs incurred therewith in the damage of property or person will be the sole responsibility of the property owner!"

The two waited. There was no answer.

"Promovendis!" called Constable Fleabo again. "Having duly warned you in advance it is now my duty to inform you that forceful entry to the premises will commence forthwith!"

Constable Fleabo heaved back and prepared to kick the door in with all his force. He took a deep breath.

Deputy Deepak raised a finger and gestured for Constable Fleabo to wait. With an apologetic shrug he reached forward and tried the doorknob.

The door opened.

Constable Fleabo grunted appreciatively. He straightened up, patted his uniform, and entered the house. Deputy Deepak followed dutifully.

Theo listened from the hiding place up the hill. It had been a mad dash to grab his project—pollens, instruments, bugs, and all —in time to duck out the back door before the policemen came in. Who knew what kind damage they might do. Of course, the incriminating doll head had been his top priority.

He stayed where he was even after the police had gone. They'd be back without a doubt. The next time he might not be so lucky to see them in time. He decided to stay in the hiding place until his father came home.

In the mean time, he had what he needed to affix the head. He activated his creation and observed the bugs settle into their labyrinthine patterns. The automaton wriggled contentedly.

Night fell, and Rudy did not return. He must be out research-ing nocturnal insects, thought Theo. Or maybe he was collecting fireflies or bioluminescent fungi from the meadow lands west of Mossville, which were much easier to find in the dark. There were plenty of good reasons why Rudy might be out at night. It wasn't like his father to leave for so long without telling him, but Theo knew Rudy could be absentminded about other things when he focused on his work.

All the same, Theo became increasingly uneasy as the night wore on. At some point he fell asleep, but when he woke in the morning with his face in the leaves he did not feel rested at all.

Theo peeked through the window of Fionn's Hardware. He wondered why he had bothered to come. Of course his father hadn't spent a day and a half in the hardware store. He thought of asking the shopkeeper, but decided it was too risky to be seen.

The city center was a dangerous maze. There seemed to be more policemen out than usual. He thought he caught a glimpse of Deputy Deepak talking to an elderly lady in front of a bakery.

Theo kept himself concealed among the shoppers and peeked around corners before crossing streets. Caution slowed him down as he tried to get to all the places he thought of where his father might have been.

But there was no sign of Rudy at the hardware store, or the craft shop, or the butcher shop where he occasionally stopped for sausages. There was no sign of him at the barber shop, which he visited once every blue moon when his hair became unwieldy. Theo peeked in at the tailor where his father had bought a vest and trousers two years previously, but without much optimism. Rudy didn't often shop for clothes. Theo checked a locksmith, a watch repair shop, and a cobbler shop but saw no trace of his father. The search felt increasingly futile. There wasn't much else his father did in town.

A flier posted over the wooden cobbler shop signboard caught Theo's attention. A public announcement of an extraordinary new invention was to take place today at two o'clock in the main square. He looked up at a nearby street clock. It was nearly two now. His curiosity piqued, Theo made his way to the square.

A small stage was set up in the town square not far from the base of the Suction-Flux Hydro Debogilator. Upon the stage an object draped in a white cloth stood atop a table. A crowd had gathered of mostly casual onlookers taking a moment from shopping or returning to work from an extended lunch. Ballhatchet and Dooley stood in front of the stage. Constable Fleabo and Deputy Deepak stood off to the side observing the crowd.

Theo watched from a doorway in a nearby alley. He was well hidden, but his view was obscured. The center of the stage was concealed by a cluster of scaffolding. He could see the table, but he could not see the object on top of it. He could only see a small corner of the crowd.

Among the passersby Theo could not see were Valerie Digniggleby and her mother, who were once again out shopping for clothes. They had just finished having cupcakes at a pastry shop on the square. They were just around the corner from where Theo hid when the announcement began.

Mr. Cess appeared on the stage in front of a bulky microphone.

"Ladies and Gentlemen!" he said. "Welcome to a most extraordinary demonstration! What I am about to show you is a result of years of painstaking effort and studious research. The creation I will unveil to you represents a turning point in mankind's history, at which man has finally truly mastered the beasts and harnessed the power of nature to do his bidding!"

A hush came over the crowd.

"I give to you…" continued Cess, dramatically yanking the cloth covering away from the object on the platform. "The Insect-Powered Engine!"

Theo's eyes widened. What could this possibly mean?

The rest of the crowd reacted much less excitedly. In fact, there was not much reaction at all. People looked at each other with puzzled expressions.

"An engine that is powered by insects," emphasized Mr. Cess.

A decidedly nonplussed-looking gentleman standing directly in front of the stage spoke up.

"What, bugs?" he said.

"Yes," said Mr. Cess.

"What, like, dead ones?" said the gentleman.

Mr. Cess spoke directly to the gentleman, out of range of the microphone.

"No, live ones," he said.

He returned to the microphone and continued. "Ladies and Gentlemen," he said. "A demonstration!"

Theo simply had to see this. He crept out of the doorway to the end of the alley. The scaffolding was still hiding the device. He made sure Constable Fleabo and Deputy Deepak weren't looking and he ducked into the crowd. He made his way towards the stage.

Cynthia Digniggleby had seen enough. She took Valerie by the hand.

"Come," she said. "We do not want to be party to any nonsense with insects."

"But—" protested Valerie.

"Quickly, Honey," said Cynthia. "He's going to do something disgusting."

Cess produced a jar of deep pink fluid, several bottles of powders, and a sheet of folded paper. He unfolded the paper and studied it while setting up the machine. With a metal spoon he placed several spoonfuls of flax-colored powder into a hopper at the top. Ballhatchet carried a large bellows and set it on a tripod in the front of the stage. He attached a broad metal pan. Dooley began to pour the pink fluid into the pan.

If Theo had been shocked before, he was doubly shocked now. The device had been crudely and hastily assembled, but it was his father's invention without a doubt. If that wasn't enough in itself to make him forget to stay hidden, then the quantity of at-tractant that Dooley was pouring onto the pan certainly was.

"What's he *doing*?" Theo said aloud to no-one. He squirmed past the elbows of the people around him to get a better look.

Cess gave a nod, and Ballhatchet brought his weight down on the bellows, sending a huge pink cloud of attractant into the air over the square.

"NO!" exclaimed Theo. "It's too much!"

Theo regretted it as soon as the words left his mouth. Cess turned towards him suddenly, bumping the jar of pink fluid which crashed to the stage. A ripple went through the crowd and all eyes turned to Theo. Ballhatchet and Dooley assumed Kung-Fu posi-tions on the stage.

Constable Fleabo sprang into action.

"Hey, you!" shouted Constable Fleabo. He started after Theo, who dove back into the crowd.

Over the ridge beyond the valley, a dark cloud began to rise.

Cynthia dragged Valerie away quickly, an expression of dis-gust on her face. Valerie craned her neck to see over her shoulder, fascinated by the mayhem.

Constable Fleabo and Deputy Deepak gave pursuit through the crowd, losing sight of Theo as he submerged and scrambled among the legs of the onlookers, then catching sight of him again as he popped up elsewhere to get his bearings.

"Ballhatchet! Dooley!" called Cess. "Help the officers!"

Ballhatchet and Dooley waded into the confused crowd. Theo ducked and covered his head to avoid being trampled.

Theo spotted an opening among the legs. It was a clear shot to the alleyway leading out of the square. He dashed towards it.

It was too late. Ballhatchet's huge hand grabbed his collar and raised him above the heads of the crowd. Theo's legs ran helplessly in the air.

"Got him!" hollered Ballhatchet proudly.

Constable Fleabo hurried to Ballhatchet's side, out of breath and panting.

A buzzing sound had become audible. If it hadn't been for the commotion, someone would surely have noticed the sky had also darkened appreciably.

"You, my boy, are under arrest!" declared Constable Fleabo. "Deputy Deepak, handcuff this scofflaw!"

Deputy Deepak raised the cuffs.

"That's my dad's invention!" shouted Theo.

"Sit still there a minute, son," said Deputy Deepak. "I don't want to pinch you."

Deputy Deepak snapped one cuff onto Theo's left wrist.

The buzzing grew into a roar.

"Huh?" said Deputy Deepak, looking up.

A massive, black swarm of insects almost as big as the city center itself slammed the town square with such force the ground shook.

Sheer chaos erupted. Most of the onlookers had been knocked clear off their feet and now scrambled on the ground to escape the onslaught of bugs. People ran blindly, reeling and spitting bugs from their mouths and batting at the bugs in their eyes.

For a moment, Theo was as overwhelmed as anybody else, but he came to his senses quickly. He groped around in his satchel for a few seconds then pulled out a canister of white powder. He popped off the lid and shook the contents out in front of himself. The bugs parted before him, creating a shifting, wobbling corridor in the wake of the powder. He shook the powder out as he went, making his way slowly out of the swarm. Once clear, he broke into a run and disappeared down the alley without looking up.

Valerie saw him go. She had recognized him when Ballhatchet had held him up, and her impulses could no longer be contained. She pulled free of her mother's hand and raced into the alley after Theo.

Cynthia turned in time to see her disappear around the corner.

"Valerie!" she shrieked, just before being engulfed in a cloud of bugs.

Chapter 11
The Bug Baby Revealed

THEO LAY PANTING, SPRAWLED on the ground in the shelter in the woods. The loose end of the handcuff lay beside his left hand. He was more lonely and confused than ever. What was going on? Where was his father? How did those men get the plans to the engine?

He looked over at his creation. The insects buzzed contentedly.

"At least you're safe," he said.

A rustling sound came from outside the shelter. Startled, Theo looked up to see a clump of branches thrust aside. The sun spilled into his eyes and he squinted up at the back-lit figure of Valerie standing over him.

"Who are you talking to?" demanded Valerie.

Unconsciously, Theo glanced down at where his creation sat concealed in the shadow of the shelter. Valerie's eyes followed his.

"Bea!" she exclaimed. She pulled another bundle of branches out of her way and charged into the shelter.

Theo jumped to his feet.

"No!" he shouted. He reached out to stop her.

Valerie grabbed Theo's wrist and in a single deft movement flipped him over her shoulder. Theo landed flat on his back with a loud thump. He moved his mouth like a fish out of water as he struggled to get his breath.

"You picked the wrong girl to mess with," said Valerie. "I've been doing ballet since I was two."

Theo managed to inhale.

"That's... not... ballet!" he gasped.

"My ballet teacher knows karate," she said. "Don't tell my mom. Now give me back my doll!"

She reached out to grab the creation. Suddenly, she stopped.

The doll was moving. What's more, it was covered with bugs. Covered wasn't even the word. It was engulfed in bugs, filled with bugs—it almost seemed to be *made of* bugs. It certainly didn't look much like the Baby Doll Bea her mother had given her.

"What is… this?" she asked, crinkling her nose.

"It's none of your business," said Theo, who had managed to raise himself to all fours and was beginning to breathe normally again.

"What have you done with my doll?" demanded Valerie.

Theo shook his head.

"It's not your doll anymore," he said.

The two of them watched the creature move. Valerie's jaw dropped slowly.

Narrow streams of green aphids wound up and down the copper and steel skeleton as though circulating through invisible veins and arteries, from the torso to the fingertips and toes. Clouds of gnats clustered around the joints, tapping out skittering patterns on tiny switches that lined the limbs. Moths, cicadas, and crickets tugged tiny fibers attached to tiny networks of pulleys to create the effect of flexing muscles.

The porcelain head of Baby Doll Bea stared back at the two children. The top of the head was open to expose the delicate clockwork of the head, from which hundreds of butterflies, moths, and bees emerged on threadlike tethers that looked like a thick head of wildly writhing hair. The flashes of fireflies emanated from the doll's eye holes, creating an uncanny sense of intelligence.

"What is it?"

"It's an automaton," said Theo. "I made it."

"It's weird!" said Valerie.

"Shut up! It's not weird," said Theo.

"Anyway, it's still mine," said Valerie. "You still have to give it back."

She paused for a moment, looking at the creature.

"Her name's Bea," she said.

"No way," said Theo. "You stay away from it. And it's not a 'her' anyway."

"What are you going to do to stop me?" challenged Valerie. "Would you hit a girl?"

Theo wasn't sure he'd hit a girl, and he was even less sure he wanted to try it with this one.

"Don't touch it," he said as forcefully as he could.

"You're going to get in so much trouble," said Valerie, narrowing her eyes. "Wait till I tell."

"No!" cried Theo. "You can't tell! They'd take it away and throw me in jail!"

"You stole my doll!" Valerie charged. "You belong in jail! I hope they throw away the key!"

Theo went pale.

"They'll destroy it!" he said.

Valerie stared at the creature, mesmerized by its strange, infantile movements.

"Can it... see us?" she said.

"In a way," said Theo. "The bugs can see."

"It's just a bunch of bugs?" said Valerie.

"Not exactly," said Theo. "The bugs are... interacting. I set up patterns for them to follow using special chemicals. When they follow their patterns they influence each other and..."

Theo gestured at the creature.

"Behavior arises," he said. "You could think of it as a brain made of bugs."

"That's disgusting," said Valerie.

She cocked her head.

"Is it smart?" she asked.

"I don't really know yet," said Theo. "I think it's learning."

Theo looked at Valerie with pleading eyes.

"Listen," he said. "If you tell on me they'll take it away. They don't know how to take care of it. It would die for sure."

"Does it eat?" asked Valerie.

"Kind of," said Theo. "It's complicated though. I need to give it the right pollens. If the mix isn't right, or it gets exposed to the wrong scents, it will have problems."

Valerie considered.

"Fine," she said. "I'll keep your secret. On one condition. It's *half mine*. And it's a *she*. And her name is *Bea*."

"That's three conditions!" cried Theo.

"I meant three," said Valerie. "Deal or not?"

Theo was gutted. He gave Valerie's offer a moment of anguished thought, but could see no alternative.

"Okay," he said. "But no telling anybody, *no matter what*."

Valerie approached Bea.

"Actually, you're not so weird looking once a person gets used to you, are you?" she said. She looked at Bea's mechanical body. "But you do need clothes."

Theo watched in helpless horror. What had he gotten himself into now?

Valerie turned to Theo and gestured to the handcuffs dangling from his wrist.

"You should get rid of those," she said. "It sets a bad example."

In the aftermath of the swarm, the handful of people who remained in the town square shooed off the last few clumps of bugs. Everyone was covered with bites and welts.

"Get that boy," said Cess.

"Yes sir," said Dooley.

"I've got a plan to get him, sir," said Ballhatchet.

"Shut up, Ballhatchet," said Dooley.

Ballhatchet cast a hurt glance at Dooley.

"Why? It's a good idea," he said. "Believe me!"

"I don't care how you do it," growled Cess. "Just—"

A beetle poked its head out from Cess's nostril.

"Uh, boss—" began Ballhatchet.

Cess sneezed and the beetle popped out. He winced in fury as it flew away.

Chapter 12
Of Vigilant Minions and Clerical Discontent

A LOT OF THINGS in Rudy's workshop were not within easy reach for Theo. On the highest shelf against the wall over the workbench, among bottles of screws and fasteners, Theo spotted what he was looking for: a brown glass jar with a worn masking tape label across it that read BOBBY PINS.

Valerie had been right about one thing. It was a good idea to get the handcuffs off as soon as possible. Theo still expected Rudy to return home at any moment, with apologies for his absentmindedness and a perfectly reasonable explanation for where he'd been. Theo didn't think his own status a fugitive from the law needed to be the first thing they talked about.

Theo climbed onto the workbench and reached for the bottle. The shelf was just a bit too high. He strained, placing his other hand on a lower shelf to give himself a boost.

That was a mistake.

The lower shelf gave way under his weight. The shelf pivoted on its bracket and the far end swung up. Bottles of powders and goop sailed into the air and crashed down around Theo as he tumbled to the floor. A jar of deep pink leonore extract smashed against the corner of the workbench and splattered all over Theo.

Spilled leonore extract! Theo acted quickly. The window of the workshop was open. Theo dashed over and slammed it shut. He pushed rags against the cracks around the frames, to keep the scent of the leonore from escaping.

He grabbed a mop and a canvas sack and hastily set to work getting the messed cleaned up.

When Theo had stuffed the last of many pungent, sopping rags into the bag he pulled the drawstring shut, wrapped the bag up in blankets and buried it in the bottom of an old trunk in the corner of the workshop.

He looked at the handcuff around his wrist. The leonore extract had hardened and darkened to a deep maroon. They keyhole, hinges, and latch areas were caked thick and solid with the substance.

"Oh, great," said Theo to himself. He'd need more than a bobby pin for this.

He wrapped a rag tightly around his wrist, concealing the handcuffs. This would have to do for now.

He went to the window and peeked out. The air around the house was clear.

Ballhatchet and Dooley walked together up the tree-lined country road towards the Promovendis house.

"What I have in mind is this," said Ballhatchet. "We knock on the door and talk in a little old lady voice and say we're selling jam."

"Why would we do that?" said Dooley.

"To gain the element of surprise, of course," said Ballhatchet. "Wouldn't you be surprised if you opened the door thinking you were going to get some jam and saw the two of us?"

"I don't see why we have to say anything," said Dooley. "we just knock on the door and grab the kid when he answers."

"Well, what if he says 'Who's there?'" said Ballhatchet.

"Then we kick the door in and grab him," said Dooley.

"We'd blow our cover doing that," said Ballhatchet. "Little old ladies can't kick doors in."

Dooley shot Ballhatchet an irritated look.

When they reached the house, the door was open and nobody was in.

Cess returned to the patent office in a foul mood, the odd gnat still emerging here and there from the folds of his clothing. What he saw at the office did nothing to improve his spirits.

A picket line had formed in front of the patent office. The clerks marched back and forth carrying signs with disgruntled messages. "On Strike," and "Give Us A Raise," read the signs.

"Wonderful," growled Cess as he stormed through the picket line.

He met Felix in the waiting area of the patent office. Felix was carrying a tray of cups of coffee. A handful of patent applicants sat waiting for their interviews.

"Who's behind all this?" demanded Cess.

Felix took a deep breath.

"I am, sir," he said. "I think it's about time we had a raise."

"A raise? About time?" Cess stared at Felix as though the words were entirely foreign.

"Sir, I've shown you the numbers," Felix said, trying hard to keep his voice steady. "We may not be worth much to you, but we've got mouths to feed."

"So what does all this mean?" said Cess, gesturing contemptuously towards the picket line. "You're not going to work? What about these people? Not a thought for them?"

Cess pointed to the disheveled collection of oddballs sitting in the waiting area, clutching their stacks of devices and plans.

"We realize it's an inconvenience," said Felix.

Cess spun on his heel and spoke into the face of a thickly bearded applicant.

"You! What do you do for a living?" he demanded.

"Me?" said the applicant, jarred from a daydream. "Uh, I hope one day to market my head-mounted mechanical toothpick. At the moment I sleep in a municipal bicycle shed to keep costs down."

"How would you like to work in the fast-paced, thrilling world of patent administration?" said Cess.

"I suppose it's worth a try," said the applicant.

Cess turned to Felix.

"Meet your replacement," he said. "You're fired. And on your way out tell that gaggle of reprobates out there they've got thirty seconds to reclaim their seats."

Felix's jaw dropped. Cess stepped into the elevator.

"Mouths to feed!" he spat.

In the secret shelter, Theo watched nervously as Valerie carried on a one-sided conversation with his creation.

"Can you talk?" said Valerie. "My name is Valerie. Can you say Valerie?"

"It can't talk," said Theo.

"*She* can't talk," corrected Valerie. "We had a deal. And anyway, how do you know?"

"Fine, she can't talk," said Theo. "I know because I built it... her."

Valerie took a bow from her hair and dangled it in front of Bea.

"Do you like toys?" she said.

The bugs swarming around Bea's head reacted to the movement of the bow. A ripple of movement percolated through the swarm and made its way to Bea's eyes and neck. Bea's head followed the movement of the bow.

"Look," cried Valerie, "she sees it!"

Theo watched. Indeed, Bea's flickering gaze appeared to follow the bow. Her mechanical hand twitched.

Valerie swung the bow back and forth. Bea's head turned in jerky, uncertain movements.

"She's trying to follow it," said Valerie.

It seemed so. Theo felt a rush of excitement. There was no doubt Valerie had a way with the automaton—with *Bea*. Valerie was bringing out behavior Theo had only seen hints of up till now.

Bea's hand quivered, half extended.

"Look," said Valerie. "She wants to hold it!"

Theo looked skeptical. Bea's arm swayed.

"Yes, see?" said Valerie. "She's trying to grab it."

Valerie reached forward to help. She took Bea's wrist in her hand.

"Like this," said Valerie.

Theo saw the bugs react before he could even make a sound. "Don't!" he shouted.

It was too late. A hornet broke free of the swarm and landed on Valerie's hand. It thrust its stinger into the flesh of her thumb.

A stone's throw down the hill, Ballhatchet and Dooley poked around the Promovendis house. Strangely, it seemed as if somebody had already ransacked the house before them.

"My theory in a situation like this is you think, 'where would I be if I was the thing I was looking for?'" Ballhatchet ventured.

"Okay, then," said Dooley. "Where would you be?"

"Well, I'd be trying to hide," said Ballhatchet. "But I can't think of any good places. If it was me we'd have probably found me already."

"That's a real helpful theory, Ballhatchet," said Dooley.

"I never said it was a silver bullet," said Ballhatchet.

They looked around the house halfheartedly. There was a whole lot of junk, but nothing very interesting. They opened cupboards and closets and checked under the beds.

"My theory is there's nobody here," said Dooley.

Ballhatchet shrugged. They turned to leave.

Just then a scream pierced the air.

Moments later, Ballhatchet and Dooley crouched in the woods just off the path. Their view into the secret shelter was obscured by leaves and branches, but they could see the children clearly enough.

"We got him!" whispered Ballhatchet.

"Not so fast," said Dooley. "You see who that is?"

It took a moment for Ballhatchet to place the face. When he did, his eyes widened with surprise.

The boy was holding the Digniggleby girl's hand. She was sobbing.

"What's he doing to her?" he said.

"I don't know," said Dooley. "Hang on…"

Both the children looked towards a corner of the shelter that was out of sight from where Ballhatchet and Dooley were.

"Is there someone else there?" wondered Dooley.

The boy took a spoonful of powder from a jar. He reached cautiously with the spoon towards the hidden corner of the shelter, extending his arm as far as he could reach. He shook out the contents of the spoon and stepped back.

"He's cooking something!" whispered Ballhatchet.

"I don't think so," said Dooley.

The two children stared at the corner of the shelter.

Something shiny and metallic moved into view. Ballhatchet and Dooley squinted to make out what it was. In a moment it was clear. It was a mechanical hand. The hand extended smoothly towards the children.

The two children looked at each other. They seemed surprised. The boy nodded to the Diniggleby girl, who slowly extended her own hand. She held a large purple bow.

Ballhatchet and Dooley gasped at what they saw next. The owner of the mechanical hand leaned forward into view. It reached out and gently took the bow.

"Holy—Ballhatchet, are you seeing what I'm seeing?" said Dooley.

"I'm seeing something weird," said Ballhatchet.

"That thing isn't human, is it," said Dooley.

"I don't think so," said Ballhatchet.

"We gotta tell Mr. Cess about this," said Dooley.

"Why don't we just grab 'em all?" said Ballhatchet.

"Are you crazy? That's the mayor's kid!" said Dooley. "We gotta have a delicate touch here."

Dooley squinted again in the direction of the secret shelter. He looked around to be sure not to forget the spot.

"We know where they are now," he said. "Let's get back."

A short while later, the two of them sat in Cess's office and tried to explain what they had seen.

"A *baby*?" said Cess.

"Like some kind of robot, or a puppet or something," said Dooley.

"With those bugs you like!" interjected Ballhatchet. "Like the toaster thing from the demonstration."

Cess did not conceal his irritation.

"Firstly, I don't especially like the bugs," he said. "Secondly, it was not a toaster."

"It was kind of hard to tell what it was, sir," said Ballhatchet.

"Ballhatchet, how about you just shut up," said Dooley. Then to Cess he said, "I made the call to wait and get the kid and the thing later."

"So you did," said Cess.

He had to admit his curiosity was piqued.

In the living room of the Mayoral Mansion Cynthia Dignig-gleby sat, disheveled and welted with bug bites. She slapped an itch on her wrist repeatedly.

"That man is a *menace!*" she said. "You see what he's trying to do, don't you?"

Mayor Digniggleby wanted very much to comfort his wife, but he wasn't especially good at it. He stood stiffly a few feet away and gently petted the air with one hand to calm her.

"I, uh, Cynthia sweetheart—" he began. "Uh, no. What's he trying to do?"

"He's trying to take over your position!" she exclaimed. "Isn't it obvious? You became the mayor because the people were grateful for your invention! Now he's trying to upstage you with that vile bug contraption!"

"Now, that's not a very charitable way of looking at it," said Digniggleby. "Mr. Cess has always supported me."

"Supported you indeed," seethed Cynthia. "Like a tent-pole! When will you get a spine of your own?"

At that moment, Valerie walked in the front door. Cynthia leaped up and raced over to hug her.

"Darling! I'm so glad you're home!" said Cynthia. "I've been positively distracted with worry!"

"I want a new doll," said Valerie.

"Why, of course, honey," said Cynthia.

"I want to pick it myself," said Valerie.

Cynthia shot Digniggleby one more angry look.

"Let's go shopping right now, honey," she said to Valerie. "Daddy has work to do."

Chapter 13
Searchers and Finders

THE NEXT MORNING, RUDY had still not returned. Theo ate what was left of a bottle of yogurt and a handful of walnuts. There were enough coins in the kitchen money jar that he'd be able to take care of himself for a while, but he had no doubt now. Something was wrong.

Theo tried not to fear the worst. If not in the city, his father could be anywhere. Collecting the ingredients for his work required him to visit all kinds of wild places, and some of them were dangerous. Ferocious animals, poisonous insects, and overprotective property owners were common hazards. Theo shuddered when he thought of the wild boars of Bastable Wood to the northeast of Mossville. They were notoriously protective of their truffles. Theo had gotten too close for comfort more than once while collecting spores there.

It was out of the question to go to the authorities when he himself was on the run. It wouldn't help anybody for him to be thrown in jail, even for a short time. In any case, Theo didn't have much confidence in the abilities of the Mossville police. If they couldn't even catch an eleven-year-old boy what use could they possibly be?

Theo would have to be his own one-man search party. He'd go to the places his father went and he'd find him one way or another. Theo only hoped that wherever his father was, he would be all right there for a while.

The only question was where to look first.

One thing Theo did know was that he needed leonore extract. Both Bea and his father's engines used a lot of that. The leonore extract attracted the bugs and stimulated the aphids to secrete their honeydew, which was the basis of the whole system. Theo's supply was almost gone and the only reserve in the house had been in the bottle he'd splashed all over the workshop.

There wasn't much dangerous about the leonore fields. It was hard to imagine his father running into trouble just collecting flowers. But it was a place his father went frequently, and with the supply low it would have been a likely place to go.

Theo left Bea resting peacefully in the secret shelter. The bugs seemed stable, orbiting and circulating smoothly. He collected Buford the Toad from the windowsill enclosure and headed towards the leonore fields.

It was about a three mile walk from the house in the opposite direction of town. Most of the way was woods. The sun peeked through the trees. Theo carried Buford in a large wooden bucket. The toad clung to the rim, watching the scenery.

The leonore fields were in full bloom, a blanket of pink so bright it seemed to glow in the sunshine. Theo scanned the rolling fields as far as he could see. There was no sign of anyone there.

Bea would be needing the leonore extract soon. He set to work picking the blossoms.

Ballhatchet and Dooley peeked through the foliage at the peacefully reclining Bea. Ballhatchet held a large potato sack.

"Here's my idea," whispered Ballhatchet. "I say we lure it out with sausages."

"What the heck are you talking about?" said Dooley. "That's the stupidest thing I ever heard."

"I don't know why you always think my ideas are stupid," said Ballhatchet. "Babies love sausages."

"Where'd you get the idea babies love sausages?" said Dooley.

"Everybody knows that," said Ballhatchet.

"First of all, Ballhatchet, that's a bunch of hooey," said Dooley. "And it doesn't matter anyway because that thing is no baby. It's a doll head for Pete's sake. What's it gonna do with a sausage?"

"Eat it of course," said Ballhatchet.

"Did you bring sausages?" asked Dooley.

"No," said Ballhatchet.

Dooley rolled his eyes.

"Here's what we're gonna do," he said. "We're going to grab it and stick it in the sack. Ready?"

With a crash, Ballhatchet and Dooley barged through the branches of the shelter. Bea flailed in reaction, her movements awkward and jerky. The insects' flights became irregular and clouds of insects spread haphazardly out from her joints and belly. The halo of bugs that encircled her head shifted into wild, irregular shapes.

Dooley grabbed Bea. Her body twitched and kicked violently at his touch. The circulating swarms of insects clustered and unclustered spasmodically, loosening into shapeless clouds then tightening into knots around Dooley.

"I got it!" he yelled.

"Open up the bag!"

Ballhatchet fumbled to find the mouth of the potato sack. It took him a few seconds to realize he was holding it upside down.

"Ballhatchet!" hollered Dooley.

Ballhatchet struggled to turn the potato sack around and hold it open. All at once, a cloud of insects exploded from Bea's midsection and her body went limp. A thick black cloud of wasps, moths, cicadas and gnats attacked Dooley with full force.

"Gaah!" cried Dooley, dropping Bea and falling to his knees.

Ballhatchet lunged towards Bea.

"I got it, I got it!" he shouted.

A second cloud of bugs split off from the first and swarmed over Ballhatchet.

"Ow! Ow!" he cried.

The men swung their arms wildly, helplessly batting at the thousands of bugs that tormented them. Dooley gestured pathetically to retreat. He walked on his knees almost blindly, his hands occupied with waving and wiping the bugs. Finally he managed to find his feet and he broke into a run. Ballhatchet followed. The two of them ran and ran until the clouds of insects around them had thinned and disappeared.

"Blasted bugs!" said Dooley. "Now what are we gonna do?"

"If we had some sausages—" began Ballhatchet.

"Ballhatchet!" exclaimed Dooley. But he had nothing else to say.

It was late afternoon when Theo returned with a full bucket of leonore blossoms. There had been no trace of his father any-where near the leonore fields. Theo felt dejected and afraid. He put Buford back into his enclosure and left the leonore in the workshop for processing later. Then he headed up to the shelter.

Valerie was already there in the shelter with Bea. Bea was dressed in a purple silk dress with white lace and gold-threaded trim. For a moment, Theo was too surprised by the clothing to put his finger on what else was wrong.

"Isn't she beautiful!" said Valerie. "She let me dress her! I think she's starting to like me. She didn't fuss at all."

But Theo just stared. An expression of horror fell over his face. Bea was strangely limp. The buzzing of the bugs was faint and uneven and the clouds around her were much sparser and slower than usual.

"What's this?" he said. "What happened here?"

"We had a deal!" insisted Valerie in a hurt voice. "You said I could dress her!"

"Not that," said Theo.

Theo looked around the shelter. A section of the shelter had been completely destroyed. Branches were broken and leaves lit-tered the ground. There were footprints of large shoes and gashes in the dirt floor of the shelter. Something violent had happened here.

Theo reached down and picked up a few small mechanical parts that had been knocked off Bea in the scuffle.

Valerie too now saw what Theo was talking about. She chas-tised herself silently for not having noticed sooner. Theo saw con-fusion and fear in her eyes.

"When did you get here?" asked Theo.

"Just a little while ago," said Valerie. "I just wanted to put the dress on and surprise you."

"How is she?" asked Theo.

They both looked at Bea.

"I don't know," said Valerie. Her voice was almost a whisper. "I just thought she was sleepy."

Theo crouched down. From his bag he took a palette of powders and gels and began to apply them to Bea. Gradually, the buzzing became more even and the bugs flew more smoothly. Bea turned her head back and forth groggily. Her body trembled.

"She needs more bugs," said Theo. "Especially aphids. We need to take her out a bit. I think she can collect them without my having to draw a swarm if we give her some time."

"What if someone sees her?" asked Valerie. "What if they come after her again?"

"We'll have to be careful," said Theo. "I think I know a place."

Theo lifted Bea and led them through the woods towards the southern tip of Gurwell's field. They came to a patch of wild grass set into the hillside concealed by trees and rocks.

Theo set Bea down and dabbed her lightly with the remnants of the leonore extract from his pack. With a dropper, he applied a yellowish fluid to the clockwork switches of her head. A drop of the fluid ran down the side of Bea's face. Valerie took a handkerchief from her purse and reached forward to wipe it off. Bea turned her head away from the handkerchief in annoyance.

"I brought some sandwiches," said Valerie. "Want one?"

She handed Theo a roll filled with meat and alfalfa sprouts.

Little by little, bugs came from the woods, the field, and the valley below. They circled Bea in a sparse cloud. Bea's trembling began to subside.

Valerie held out her fingers for Bea to grab. Bea's shaky fingers closed around Valerie's. Bea crouched on her haunches and pushed as Valerie tried to help her to her feet.

"She's trying," said Valerie.

Theo spooned several tiny spoonfuls of flax-colored powder onto platforms extending from Bea's knees. A flurry of gnats from the surrounding cloud clustered around Bea's knees and joined the ever more rapidly circulating streams of her legs.

Suddenly, Bea's grip on Valerie's fingers tightened and, in a fluid motion, Bea straightened her legs and stood. Valerie coaxed her as Theo watched, intrigued by Valerie's rapid progress with Bea.

Bea took a step.

"You hold one hand," said Valerie to Theo. She held Bea's right hand and Theo took the left.

With Valerie and Theo on either side, Bea took a few more steps, tentative at first, then increasingly confident. The three of them walked halfway across the grassy patch like this, one slow step after another.

Bea stood still. She swayed slightly back and forth. Theo and Valerie looked at each other. Bea seemed to be balanced. Slowly, they let go of her hands.

She stood by herself for a few seconds, then toppled backwards but stopped midair. She hovered in at an angle, seeming to defy gravity as the bugs held her body up and eventually righted it. Then she took a step on her own.

Preoccupied though he was about his father, Theo could scarcely contain his excitement at seeing Bea walk. He did not realize how widely he was smiling until his eyes met Valerie's.

"She's getting pretty good, isn't she!" said Valerie.

They played with Bea as the sun went down. She improved rapidly and soon she was able to run from one of them to the other. She stumbled often, but most times the bugs caught her before she landed. The other times she tumbled face first into the soft grass, but rose up undeterred and continued to play.

By the time the sun had set, she could do most of what a small child could do and a few other things as well. She could jump up and hover in the air as high as Theo's shoulders, supported by the bugs. Theo watched her increasingly graceful movements. At moments he felt he could hardly believe it had been he himself who created her.

The three of them were all tired and in relatively good spirits as they walked up the path towards the secret shelter. From time to time Bea stopped to pick up rocks and leaves.

It was Bea who stopped at the mailbox.

"What's she doing?" asked Theo.

Valerie shrugged. "She's just distracted."

Bea crouched down and picked up something white. She held it up proudly and ran happily towards Valerie.

"What do you have?" said Valerie.

It was a torn white envelope.

"That's just garbage," said Valerie. "Give it to me."

Theo stepped closer to look.

"Let me see that," he said.

Written across the front of the envelope was his father's name. The return address was stamped **MOSSVILLE MUNICIPAL OFFICE OF PATENT REGISTRATION AND PROCESSING.**

Theo tried to think of what it could mean. His father's disappearance, the demonstration in the town square, and now this. He could make no sense of it. But he certainly knew where he had to look next.

"I need you to take care of her tomorrow," he said.

"Why? Where will you be?" asked Valerie.

"I have to find my dad," said Theo.

Valerie gestured at Theo's bag.

"But I don't know anything about all that stuff," she said.

"You have to learn," said Theo. "I can teach you."

Valerie looked uneasily at Bea.

"She's half yours, you know," said Theo.

Chapter 14
The Catastrophic Consequences of
Snacking on Duty

CYNTHIA DIGNIGGLEBY WAS IN HER BATHROBE and curlers making toast when cleared the stairs in two strides and dashed out the front door.

"Valerie?"

"I'll be back late!" called Valerie. "Don't wait up!"

With that, the door slammed and Valerie was gone.

Mayor Digniggleby looked up from his oatmeal.

When Valerie arrived at the shelter, Theo was ready to leave.

"It took you long enough," said Theo.

"I'm here now," said Valerie.

Theo handed her his bag and a small, corked bottle of deep pink leonore extract.

"I made a fresh batch," he said. "This is very potent. Use it like I told you, but don't leave it exposed to the air."

Valerie nodded. "Just don't be late. My parents will start looking for me if it gets late."

"I'm not going to be late," said Theo.

Valerie scrunched her nose.

"What's *that*?" she said, pointing at a wriggling lump in Theo's breast pocket. Theo blushed.

"It's my toad," he said irritably.

Ballhatchet and Dooley sat side by side across the desk from Cess.

"Sorry to disappoint you boss," said Dooley.

"I'll live," said Cess.

"I think we need to take another approach," said Dooley.

"I've been thinking sausages," said Ballhatchet. "Or maybe grapes. But Dooley—"

"Ballhatchet, shut up," said Dooley.

"Dooley doesn't like my ideas," finished Ballhatchet.

Cess stood and walked over to the bookshelf. He took down a large jar of deep pink fluid. He placed it on the desk in front of Ballhatchet and Dooley.

"This will attract the insects," he said. "Once you've managed that, the sack should suffice."

Theo crouched behind a shrub on the corner near the entrance of the patent office and watched as Ballhatchet and Dooley walked out the front door.

"For the last time, enough about the sausages!" said Dooley.

The two men disappeared down the street.

Theo looked around to make sure nobody was watching him. He jogged over to the patent office building.

Above him, the elevator rattled. It came to rest on the ground floor. The front door of the patent office opened again and Theo dove behind one of the scaffold beams that supported the building above.

Chief Patent Administrator Horace E. Cess emerged from the building. He wore a top hat and tails and carried a gold-tipped walking stick. He puffed up his chest, tucked the walking stick under one arm, and walked down the street away from the patent office.

As soon as Cess rounded the corner Theo hoisted himself onto the beam. The beam was lined with metal pegs all the way up, and Theo could climb it as easily as climbing a ladder.

It was a long way up to the house, but the scaffolding and elevator apparatus kept him well concealed. Halfway up, Theo sat down on a shaft behind a massive flywheel to catch his breath. He peeked out from among the girders and looked out over Mossville. Even from here the view was impressive. He saw the sea of red-tiled roofs that surrounded the town square and stretched up the side of the valley to the west. The roofs became more sparse as they rose up the slope into the woods in the direction of Theo's home. To the east, the buildings ended much more abruptly, well short of the craggy black edge of the ravine beyond. Overhead, the Suction-Flux Hydro-Debogilator spanned the sky in a soaring parabola from the town square into the mist of the ravine.

Theo continued to climb. About three-quarters of the way up he reached a rickety wooden stairwell that spiraled upward around the elevator shaft. He stepped onto the stairwell. He was high enough now that there was little chance anyone would see him from the ground.

As he climbed, he passed platforms and balconies that jutted from the stairwell at odd angles. Soon he was level with the bottommost rooms of the house. A walkway ran from the stairs to the lowest floor of the house. It was scarcely more than the size of a broom closet and nuzzled up against the side of the elevator shaft. The bottom of the house was shaped something like a radish. The floors were wider as he went up, and more walkways split off from the stairs towards other doors. Ladders led to still other sets of stairs.

Theo continued upward through the bird's nest of walkways and balconies. He climbed past shuttered windows and wood-shingled gables until he reached the topmost balcony of the house. A chilly breeze ruffled his hair.

The platform he stood on was scarcely big enough for one person to stand on comfortably. At one corner of the balcony a steel pole rose up into the air. At the top of the pole a bullwheel supported a cable that stretched off eastward towards another similar pole far off in the hazy distance.

A wooden sign in the shape of an arrow pointing east hung on the railing of the balcony. It read KOOK BOG.

About ten feet below him was another platform, from which a steel maintenance catwalk extended to the nearest point of the Suction-Flux Hydro-Debogilator about fifty yards away. The catwalk was supported by struts and cables bolted to the scaffolding on the near end and to the Suction-Flux Hydro-Debogilator itself on the far end.

The city below looked like a train-set town he might have built himself when he was younger. The tower seemed to spin slowly and Theo closed his eyes to stop the vertigo.

Theo tried the door of the room adjoining the balcony. It was unlocked. He went in.

He found himself in Mr. Cess's office. Theo looked at the massive wooden desk and the tall leather chair. The room was jammed full of shelves and file cabinets and tall stacks of binders, folders, and envelopes. But although it was chockablock to bursting with documents and containers, the details of the room were meticulously tidy.

Theo walked over to a rack of tightly rolled blueprints that covered the far wall. He pulled a roll out and stretched it out on the floor.

When Ballhatchet and Dooley arrived at the secret shelter there was nobody there. Dooley held the potato sack over his shoulder and Ballhatchet carried the jar of leonore extract under his arm.

"I guess we wait," said Dooley.

They sat down on a nearby log where they could easily see anyone who approached. For a while neither of them spoke. Eventually Dooley sighed.

"It's stressful sometimes," he said.

"Mm," said Ballhatchet.

"I mean, working for Mr. Cess and all," continued Dooley. "You know how demanding he is. Don't get me wrong, I wouldn't have it any other way. He makes us rise to our potential. But I think maybe sometimes I take my stress out on you. Criticizing your ideas and all. I shouldn't do that."

"Mmm," agreed Ballhatchet.

A faint buzzing sound came through the trees.

"I think it comes down to my own insecurity about my job performance really," said Dooley. "I know I probably seem like I've always got a handle on things, but I'm human too. A lot of times I wonder whether I'm up to it, y'know? I mean, you've had my back through thick and thin, and I do appreciate that—"

Ballhatchet made a slurping sound.

Dooley turned to see Ballhatchet with his fingers in his mouth, a thick, viscous strand of leonore extract trailing from his mouth to the open bottle on his lap. Ballhatchet raised his eyebrows enthusiastically.

"What the heck are you doing?" exclaimed Dooley.

"I'm hungry!" said Ballhatchet, his lips smacking with the sticky fluid.

"That's for the bugs! Mr. Cess said to keep that shut!"

"It's really good!" said Ballhatchet. "Try some!"

The buzzing was loud now. Dooley and Ballhatchet both looked up to see a huge black swarm of insects about to hit.

"Uh-oh," said Dooley.

Valerie and Bea played together in the grass at the tip of Gurwell's field. Valerie took an old red ball from her purse.

"This used to be our dog, Finney's, but he died," she said. "Here, catch!"

She tossed the ball to Bea. The ball struck Bea square on the chest and Bea toppled over backwards.

"Oh!" said Valerie, running to help Bea up. "Maybe we should start a little easier!"

She rolled the ball to Bea a few times, coaxing Bea to catch it. After five or six tries, Bea began to reach for the ball. Soon Bea was picking up the ball and rolling it back to Valerie. Before too long, they were playing catch. When the ball flew wide of Bea a cluster of bugs spread out from Bea and pulled the ball into her reach. Bea threw the ball high and strong to Valerie.

A buzzing sound came from above. Valerie looked up to see a swarm of bugs overhead flying the direction of the Promovendis house. She dropped the ball.

"Bea!" she cried. "Come here!"

Bea tried to run towards Valerie, but her bugs had already begun to go out of control. Clusters of bugs flew away from her to join the swarm above. A spasm overtook Bea and she fell to her knees.

"Bea!"

Valerie took Theo's palette from her purse and struggled to remember what he had told her. Bea writhed and shook on the ground, her arms reaching out helplessly towards Valerie.

"Calms her down, calms her down..." said Valerie to herself. She took a spoonful of yellow powder and tried to remember where to sprinkle it. "Easy, Bea! It's okay, I've got you."

Valerie sprinkled the yellow powder on Bea's main switch panel. With a loud pop, a cloud of gnats burst from Bea's chest. Valerie fell backward in surprise and Bea's spasms became more violent than ever.

"Oh!"

Tears filled Valerie's eyes as she agonized over the palette. Bea's arms and legs levitated sickeningly, pulled in all directions by the frenzied bugs.

"Oh, I don't know!" cried Valerie.

Bea's foot swung around in a wide arc and slammed down on the palette, sending powders and liquids splashing. The spasms were horrific. It looked as though Bea was being ripped apart from within.

Valerie grabbed Bea in her arms and ran as fast as she could.

Chapter 15
An Abrupt Resolution to the Question of Custody

CESS SAT ON THE SOFA in the living room of the mayoral mansion. Across the coffee table Cynthia and Mayor Diniggleby sat stiffly together on a loveseat. On the table a tray of fancy sandwiches and three glasses of cognac laid out. Beside the tray stood Cess's reel-to-reel tape recorder. Diniggleby glanced at it uneasily.

"It is a pleasure as always," said Cess.

"Isn't it though!" said Diniggleby.

"Such a charming pleasure!" said Cynthia.

Diniggleby and Cynthia each sipped their cognac.

"Was there anything, in particular, you wanted to discuss on this pleasant afternoon, Mayor?" said Cess.

Diniggleby put down his cognac.

"Well, as a matter of fact.." began Diniggleby, trailing off. Cynthia dug her elbow into his ribcage. He cleared his throat. "I wanted to, ahem, offer you a bit of a promotion, actually."

Cess barely concealed his sneer.

"A promotion," he said.

"Well," said Diniggleby. "We—that is, *I*—were, um, thinking that... a man of your talents can't be satisfied with, ahem, clerical work. That is, administrative work. I thought maybe you'd like to leave the patent office to someone else."

"The patent office to someone else?" repeated Cess. "And what would I do?"

"Yes, well," said Diniggleby. "You would assume another, very important—really incredibly important—role."

Cess tilted his head inquisitively.

"You would be..." said Diniggleby. "That is to say, your very esteemed title would become, ahem, Official Archduke of Mossville."

"Official *what*?"

"Archduke."

Cess raised an eyebrow.

"I didn't know this city had an archduke," he said. "Official or otherwise."

"Oh, uh, yes, I see," said Digniggleby. "Well, I kind of made it up. To befit, that is, your esteemed, uh, you. That is, it's new. But it's very important."

"And what does the Official Archduke do?" asked Cess. "Officially."

Digniggleby squirmed. He turned to Cynthia for support, but she stared straight ahead at Cess, a wide, artificial smile pasted across her face. Digniggleby smiled as well.

Cess let the awkward silence linger. He took a sip of his cognac.

"I must say I am most flattered," he said at last. "And to think the very position of Official Archduke was concocted entirely for my sake. Such an unheard of honor."

Digniggleby grinned sheepishly.

"But," Cess continued, "I feel I simply could not shirk my duties as Chief Patent Administrator. It's not the kind of work that can be left to just anyone, after all."

"Ehrrr," said Digniggleby.

Cess observed Cynthia's jewelry.

"May I say, Mrs. Digniggleby, that is an extraordinary brooch."

Cynthia's face puckered indecipherably.

Before she could respond, the front door of the mansion slammed open with a crash and Valerie burst into the room sobbing. She had a strange bundle in her arms and a cloud of insects trailed her.

"Help! Daddy! Somebody help!" she cried.

Everyone in the room leaped to their feet. The butler ran in from the hall. The cloud of bugs dispersed throughout the room as Valerie put Bea down on the sofa.

"Goodness!" exclaimed Cynthia. "What on earth have you brought in?"

"She's going to die!" sobbed Valerie.

In an instant, Mr. Cess stood up and took charge.

"Remain calm!" he commanded. "Everything is under control!"

Cess turned to the butler.

"You!" he said. "Bring a bucket of boiling water!"

"Yes sir!" said the butler, and raced to the kitchen.

Cess turned to Valerie. "You! Go and fetch me ten white handkerchiefs, folded diagonally in eighths!"

Valerie nodded through her tears and ran up the stairs toward the bedrooms.

Cess turned to Cynthia. "You! Bring me five empty toilet paper tubes, glued together end to end. And firmly!" he directed.

Cynthia, puzzled, ran upstairs to do as she was told.

Cess turned to Mayor Digniggleby. "You! Bring me a balloon poodle! A red one"

"A... a balloon poodle?" said Digniggleby.

"You heard me!" said Cess. "And hurry!"

"O-okay," said Digniggleby, scurrying out the door.

Alone in the room, Cess turned slowly to where Bea lay twitching sluggishly on the sofa. He smiled mirthlessly and reached down to pick her up.

Theo sat on the floor of Cess's office surrounded by decades worth of plans. Crisp white blueprints and yellowing, stained parchments papered the floor and covered the desk.

Finding a particular device among these plans was like searching for a needle in a haystack. He had no idea how they were organized, though it was clear there was a system. Each plan was labeled with a six digit number and had a colored tag affixed, and the rows and columns of the rack were marked with a sequence of four alphanumeric symbols. But none of this held any meaning for Theo. He searched the only way he could, by pulling out as many plans as he could and going through them one by one.

It was all too easy to become distracted. There were plans for vehicles, toys, household appliances, industrial machines, even weapons. Some were childishly simple and others were mind-bendingly complex. There were electrical circuits, clockwork movements, and hydraulic systems, all drawn and labeled in painstaking detail. But one set of plans had caught his eye the moment he unrolled it. It was without a doubt the most recognizable form in all of Mossville: the massive, mighty arch of the Suction-Flux Hydro-Debogilator.

At first, it was just curiosity that made Theo look more closely at the plans. That, and the thrill of seeing such a familiar landmark amid the mess of arcane diagrams strewn over the floor. But the closer he looked at the workings of the Suction-Flux Hydro-Debogilator the more engrossed he became by its strange but ingenious logic. It was hard to square what he saw in these plans with his buffoonish perception of Mayor Digniggleby. The more Theo studied the blueprints the more convinced he became that he had seriously misjudged the mayor. It was truly a remarkable invention. Remarkable enough that Theo soon lost track of the passage of time.

In the lower left corner of the diagram a control panel was drawn, labeled *Main Control*. Another panel drawn at the apex of the arch was labeled *Manual System Override: See Further Instructions for Operation*. Theo searched the front and back of the blueprint, but could not find anything further related to the manual override.

He looked up. Across the room, a large metal box was affixed to the wall. An array of metal pipes and tubes extended from the box and down through the floor of the room. Across the front of the box, in red stenciled letters, was written **SFHD MAIN**.

Theo walked over and opened the front panel of the control box. Inside the box was a bank of buttons and switches, in the middle of which was a large Bakelite dial knob. A circular panel around the knob was color coded green, yellow and red, presumably indicating safety limits. The knob's pointer was just inside the green area.

Suddenly, a slam echoed up the elevator shaft and the engine began to hum. The sound of the elevator rumbling into motion filled the room.

In a panic, Theo scrambled to hide the mess he had made. He thrust plans and diagrams haphazardly into drawers, but it was beyond hopeless. He switched off the light and dashed out the door he had entered. No sooner had he gotten out the door than the elevator opened into the room. Cess stepped out and switched the light back on.

Theo was just about to dive onto the ladder below and take his chances climbing down when a sound from inside the room caught his attention. It was a distinctive combination of the buzzing of insects and the clicking of machinery. Theo turned slowly and pushed the door open a crack.

Theo saw Cess toss something onto the desk. It was impossible to make out the shape of the object, but the sliver of purple was unmistakeable. It was Bea's dress. And the sound Theo heard was unmistakeable too.

Suddenly, the door flew wide open and for a brief moment Theo had a full view of Bea, flung gracelessly across the desk, twitching and writhing horribly.

Theo froze.

"Bea!" he cried.

Mr. Cess stepped into the doorway and Theo's view of Bea was concealed.

"Now *this* is convenient," said Cess.

Cess reached towards the red button by the door and punched it forcefully. A whooshing sound came from over Theo's head and before he knew what was happening a large wooden bucket on the end of a steel pole swung down under his rear end and scooped him right up off the platform and into the air.

In the mayoral mansion, Valerie cried uncontrollably. Scattered on the floor of the living room were a bucket of water, a bunch of folded handkerchiefs, and an awkwardly glued pole of toilet paper rolls. Cynthia petted her daughter's hair and tried to console her.

"We'll get you another doll, sweetheart! We can find a much prettier one than that old thing!" she said.

"Bea's not a doll!" protested Valerie. "She's alive".

"Valerie, honey, it was covered with bugs! You don't want a horrible toy like that," said Cynthia.

Valerie stopped crying suddenly and stood up. She stamped her foot angrily.

"She's not a toy!" she said. "I need to get her back. He'll kill her!"

"Valerie, now, calm down," said Cynthia. "Nobody's going to kill anybody. When your father comes home he'll take care of everything."

At that, Digniggleby burst through the front door, beet-red and covered with glistening sweat. He stood in the middle of the living room, doubled over with one hand on his knee, heaving and panting. With the other hand he held up a poodle dog made from one long twisted-up red balloon. Between gasps he could barely get the words out.

"Got it!" he said.

Chapter 16
In the Land of the Kooks

THEO SOARED THROUGH THE AIR at breakneck speed, his bottom wedged tightly into the bucket seat of the Kook Bog gondola. He strained to look back over his shoulder.

"Bea! Wait!" he hollered.

The gondola flew over the patchwork of fields beyond the eastern edge of Mossville. It dipped and then rose again to clank past the next pole, then sailed over the black, craggy ridge and dropped sickeningly into the mist of the chasm beyond. Wind and moisture buffeted Theo's face.

The gondola broke through the clouds and for a few brief moments Theo could see the gas lights and low wooden buildings of a village. His eyes widened in panic as the gondola rushed straight towards the dark ground.

Fifteen feet short of hitting the ground the gondola slammed to a sickening halt, launching Theo headlong into the soft mud below. He smacked down with a belching splat.

Theo struggled to find his feet but the mud was deeper than he was tall. He managed to squirm around to get a look at the gondola hanging above him. He grabbed at it, but it was far out of his reach.

The gondola emitted a few clicks, jerked abruptly, then began to shake violently from side to side with a loud chugging sound. It slowly withdrew back up into the clouds, shaking continuously.

"Bea!" cried Theo, but there were more pressing things to worry about. He was sinking. He flailed frantically. "Help!"

The end of a long stick struck the surface of the mud beside his head. A man's voice called to him.

"Grab it!"

Theo grabbed the stick and held on tightly as he was pulled toward a wooden dock amid the sea of mud. A large, slow-moving man in worn overalls reached down and offered a meaty hand. Theo took it gratefully and scrambled onto the dock.

When Theo had caught his breath, he looked around. He was in the middle of a huge, thickly wooded swamp. Moss-covered trees and vines rose from thick mud which undulated slowly and lichen-crusted rocks poked out of the bog. Theo looked at the spot where he'd landed. His outline was still imprinted in the bubbling, swirling green scum that coated the surface. Overhead the clouds were so low he felt he could reach out and touch them. The smell of peat smoke filled the air.

A wooden walkway ran from the dock. About twenty-five yards away it intersected with a collection of other walkways, all supported by wood pilings driven into the burbling mud. In the distance through the trees yellow lights flickered.

An arrangement of tall poles dotted the swamp as far as Theo could see. Each pole was separated by a few yards in each direction from neighboring poles. The poles supported a labyrinthine network of twine that looked like an entanglement of spiderwebs over the village. The numerous lengths twine terminated at wooden racks from which dangled rows of tin cans. One of these racks was set up at the dock where Theo stood now. The man in overalls picked up one of the tin cans and spoke into it.

"Arrival," he said. "Male, about twelve years old. Four and a half feet or so. Looks like he'll have an appetite."

The man put down the tin can and turned to Theo.

"Pretty nice isn't it," said the man.

"What?" said Theo.

The man held up his stick.

"The *15-foot mid-precision remote person extractor*," he said proudly. "My baby. Reliable too! Second time this week without a hitch."

"The stick?" said Theo.

"I think of it as a helpful, lifestyle-enhancing innovation," said the man. "And job security! I'm set for life as welcoming committee with this baby."

"Welcoming committee?" repeated Theo bemusedly.

"That's me. The name's Berke. Welcome to Kook Bog."

Theo blinked. "People live here?"

Berke gestured in the direction of the lights.

"People that way. Follow the wide boardwalk straight on in," he said. "The first narrow fork off to the right goes to the bug fields. Not that you'd want to go there though. Certainly not without packing a lunch. The first fork left leads to the mushroom farm. You'll want to just keep left for that. The second walkway on the right leads to—"

"I don't need a tour," said Theo. "Just tell me how to get back."

Berke looked at Theo blankly, then glanced up at the gondola cables overhead. He furrowed his brow.

"People don't really go back," he said.

Theo opened his mouth to protest, but he had no idea what to say. A loud croak came from the mud behind him. Berke pricked up his ears and craned his neck to see where the sound had come from.

Buford sat on a lily pad a few feet away from the dock. He jumped into Theo's hands.

"That yours?" said Berke.

Theo nodded.

"That's a nice looking toad," said Berke.

Something in Berke's tone made Theo uneasy. He wasn't sure how to respond to the compliment. In any case, it was clear Berke wasn't the person to help him get out of the bog.

Theo followed the walkway toward the populated center of Kook Bog. The village was like nothing he had ever seen. It was crisscrossed with elevated boardwalks that snaked over and under each other. Some of the walkways terminated at buildings, some led to other walkways or decks, and still others led to conical gazebos which acted as hubs for the network of twine overhead.

The buildings were made of wood and built upon stilts and platforms to hold them above the bubbling mud. Over time they had sunk and settled at odd angles. Curls of smoke rose from lop-sided chimneys; some jutted out straight from the sides of houses, others extended crookedly upward. Everything looked as though it had been built by quarrelsome committees of mad visionaries. Doorknobs and window shutters were rigged with elaborate pulley and gear systems. Doors half sunken into the bog opened by unusual mechanisms: some swiveled, some slid, some folded like accordions, and some seemed to telescope into themselves.

The people had devised their own ways to get around. Most of them stayed to the boardwalks, but some used contraptions to move more freely. Several villagers waded through the mire on mechanical stilts. Another man walked across wearing pontoon shoes. Still another had harnessed himself into an elaborate rig of bungee cords and carabiners which flung him through the air from one walkway to another. A white-haired old woman flapped loudly overhead in a pedal-driven flying device that looked like a huge leather duck.

The tin-can telephone lines were everywhere. People clustered near the phone racks and chatted into the cans. The strands of twine were pulled taut on hooks throughout the town and met at the tips of the gazebo hubs. From each of the gazebo hubs the collected bundles of twine extended further to a much larger and more ornate gazebo that towered over the center of Kook Bog. This central communication gazebo bustled with activity inside. A large cylindrical switchboard stood in its center and operators sat in a circle manning the switches.

Far overhead, through a part in the clouds, Theo could see the black arc of the Suction-Flux Hydro-Debogilator extending silently across the sky.

A wild-eyed, bearded man walked past Theo with a strap around his forehead from which a dozen rear-view mirrors extended at odd angles. Another man wore a pair of hydraulic, tele-scoping stilts mounted on his belt. When he walked straight they looked like a pair of gun holsters, but when he approached a corner they extended themselves, lifted him up, turned his body in the correct new direction to walk, then put him down to continue on his way. A woman passed by with a set of head-mounted bin-aural megaphones. A destitute hobo lay against the side of a building. On his head a swiveling drinky-bird toy and a glass of water were attached to a gyroscope. When the bird tipped its beak into the water it opened a dropper and created a siphon effect that sucked whiskey out of a flask, through a coil of tubes, and into the hobo's mouth.

People were gathering on a broad deck not far from the central communication gazebo. A man's voice came through a mega-phone.

"Come one, come all! Witness the impossible!"

Theo squeezed through the crowd for a look.

A colorful, hand-painted placard was displayed on an easel. The placard read:

ASTONISHING AMPHIBIAN EXTRAVAGANZA
BRIGADIER WEISSBOTTOM S

TOAD CIRCUS

Beside the easel a broad, angled platform was set out with a complete miniature three ring circus including two trapezes, a high-wire, a unicycle, and an assortment of other props. To one side stood a peculiar agglomeration of musical instruments to which were attached an assortment of levers, see-saws, and bel-lows. In front of the platform a broad wooden vat of water was displayed. A miniature diving board extended out over the vat.

Next to the platform, the diminutive ringmaster—who Theo surmised to be the Brigadier Weissbottom of the placard—hawked the upcoming performance through the megaphone.

"Witness the astonishing amphibian extravaganza!" called Brigadier Weissbottom. "See for yourself the salientian spectacular! The most astounding show in Kook Bog!"

Brigadier Weissbottom's face was puffy and red. He sported an ample white mustache that had been painstakingly waxed and curled at the tips. His right eye was covered by a large black eye patch.

Fittingly for a circus ringmaster, he wore black top hat and a bright red and yellow high-collared, double breasted jacket with tails and epaulets, amply dotted with large gold buttons. His trousers were a cacophony of multi-colored patches tucked into scuffed black riding boots that extended most of the way up his short legs.

The crowd had gathered around the platform expectantly. Buford peered out from Theo's shirt pocket.

"Move in close! Let the short ones up front!" called Brigadier Weissbottom, who himself was shorter than anyone present, including Theo.

Brigadier Weissbottom produced what looked like a large bird cage, draped with a bright red and yellow silk cloth. He opened the front of the cloth like curtains and unlatched the door of the cage.

A row of toads hopped out of the cage and onto the platform. They appeared to be altogether ordinary toads. They varied slightly in size and color—some were brownish green, others greenish brown—but any of them could have passed for Buford in a pinch.

The toads sat in a row facing the audience and awaited their cue.

"Ladies and Gentlemen, I give you the astonishing Toad Circus!"

At that, the toads began their performance. Seven of them hopped into place on the musical contraption; one jumped up and down on a bellows attached to the mouth of the trumpet; one perched upon the valves of the trumpet and played out the melody; two others teamed up on the tuba; the fifth crawled nim- bly over the keys of the organ; the last two rode a see-saw that controlled a base drum kicker, a snare drum tap and a cymbal crash. They struck up a lively and remarkably tightly-performed waltz.

As the music played, the other toads sprang into action. They walked on their hind legs. They balanced on balls. Two of them leaped onto flying trapezes and performed a death defying routine of flips, catches, and mid-air somersaults. Others did stunts on the trampoline. One rode the miniature unicycle. Still another walked upright across the tightrope, gripping a length of wire coat hanger for balance.

"I didn't know toads could do all that," he said. He glanced down at Buford and hastily added, "No offense."

Buford also seemed duly impressed. He strained forward in Theo's pocket, his big eyes wide.

The crowd clapped and cheered the toads as they bounced, flipped, and flew through the air. Brigadier Weissbottom moved around the circle with his hat out collecting wooden coins, acorns, gears, and whatever other baubles and doohickeys the audience members happened to use as their currency. He kept a watchful eye on his toads at all times.

For the finale, an ensemble of toads dove one by one into the great vat and performed a synchronized swimming routine, while another group croaked a four part harmony of *When The Saints Go Marching In* to the accompaniment of the toads on the musi- cal instrument. A third group bounced so high above the trampo- line that they kept slipping out of view in the low clouds.

When the show was finished the toads all bowed deeply and Brigadier Weissbottom quickly ushered them back into their cage. The crowd began to disperse.

A crooked semicircle of houses and shops lined the deck. A sign hung in front of one that read *Kook Bog Inn*. A matronly woman stood in the doorway, watching the crowd. She nodded to Theo.

"You must be the new arrival," she said. "How about some dinner?"

In the excitement, Theo had almost forgotten how hungry he was. Buford's tongue flicked out and snapped up a fly, as if he too had just remembered his hunger.

The inn was crowded, full of smoke and chatter. Theo sat at the counter as the woman prepared him a meal. Beside him a man and a woman carried on a conversation through a system of flexible tubes that ran from each of their mouths directly to the other person's ears. Their conversation was inaudible outside the device but they laughed and chatted comfortably. In a corner near Theo, an old man played solitaire. He wore a strange contraption of pumps and bellows on his head. A jointed arm extended from the apparatus, at the end of which was a metal clip which held a cigar a few inches in front of the man's face. Periodically the device pumped a burst of smoke into his face.

The woman introduced herself as Dorothy. This was her inn, she explained, and had been for more years than she could remember.

Theo tucked into his meal of sausages, mushrooms and boiled potatoes. The meal was wonderful. The mushrooms were the most flavorful he'd ever eaten and the potatoes were fresh and perfectly prepared. He couldn't quite place the taste of the sausages. They were clearly not beef or pork. Theo thought perhaps they were made with chicken or duck. In any case, they were delicious.

"It's wonderful to see a boy with a healthy appetite!" said Dorothy. "You'll need it around here. There's a lot of work to be done!"

"Work?" said Theo.

Dorothy shrugged genially.

"Well, naturally, you'll need to earn your keep," she said with a warm smile. She noticed the dark pink-stained rag wrapped around Theo's wrist. "Oh dear, you're not hurt are you?"

"I'm fine," said Theo. "But I'm not staying. I have to get back to Mossville."

At those words, the inn seemed to go quiet. Dorothy pursed her lips and raised her eyebrows. Theo felt the glances of the other customers. He looked around nervously.

"What? What'd I say?" said Theo.

Other customers averted their eyes and mumbled. Eventually the man in the corner with the cigar apparatus spoke up.

"You're not going back to Mossville," said the man.

"Yes I am," said Theo.

"Makes no difference to me," said the man. "I'm just being neighborly. The sooner you rid yourself of that idea the sooner you'll settle in here."

"I'm not settling in," said Theo. "I have to go back."

The man leaned forward. "And what makes you think Mossville wants you back? There's a reason why we're all here, you know, and it's not just the mud and the mountains. You can't go where you're not needed. It's not like the rest of us didn't try." The man lowered his eyes. "Lord knows I thought the world would beat a path to my door for a hands-free cigar smoker."

"Well, I'm needed there," said Theo.

The man looked straight into Theo's eyes.

"Oh? Then what are you doing here?"

"What Harry is trying to say is that it's important to have something to offer," said Dorothy. "Something you can be appreciated for. That's why we're all here and not there."

"What I was trying to say was what I said," said Harry. "But that's another way to put it I suppose."

Other customers throughout the pub nodded and murmured in agreement. Theo scoffed.

"You people sound like my dad," he said. "All he ever wanted was to be useful. But he never knew who he wanted to be useful *to*. I don't care about making myself useful to everybody."

"Maybe you ought to listen to your dad," said the cigar man.

At that, Theo suddenly felt the weight of all that had happened in the last few days. Where *was* his dad? What were they doing to Bea? How would he ever get out of this miserable mud pit? Theo felt for a moment that if he spoke again he would burst into tears, so he said nothing. He blinked a few times and went back to eating his meal.

"You can stay here tonight," said Dorothy. "Don't worry about earning your keep at this point. It's hard to be new. It's not so bad once you get used to it."

Theo just nodded. He was far too tired to argue. There was no point mentioning he had no intention of getting used to anything here.

The bedroom was simple and a little bit dingy, but the bed was cozy and piled high with blankets and quilts. In the middle of the ceiling a bare light bulb hung on a cord. At its base was a miniature generator connected to a small water-wheel driven by droplets of water from a crack in the ceiling. The room brightened and dimmed with each drip. Theo turned off the light and soon fell fast asleep.

He wasn't sure how long he had slept when he was awoken by the feeling of something small and damp slapping on his face. He opened his eyes to see the figure of Buford the Toad just inches away from his nose. He sat up abruptly. Buford hopped to the floor into a wedge of orange light from a street lamp outside.

"What are you doing?" Theo whispered, annoyed.

Buford hopped to the window and onto the sill.

"Get down from there," said Theo. "You're going to fall out the window."

An agonized croak split the night air. Theo squinted at Buford, but the toad had not moved. Another croak came from the direction of the window. It wasn't Buford.

Theo crawled out of bed and went to the window. He looked down at walkway behind the inn. A door was open below and the smell of cooking food wafted up. In the doorway Dorothy stood haggling with a diminutive figure on the walkway. Even without his ringmaster get-up, Theo recognized Brigadier Weissbottom immediately.

"This one here is hard to part with," he said. "Used to be able to do three somersaults and a twist on the trampoline. Too fat to perform now though. Still, there's a lot on those legs."

Theo gasped. Brigadier Weissbottom held a large toad up to the light by its feet. Dorothy took the toad, looked it over, and dropped it into a basket. The basket was already nearly full of other toads. On the walkway beside the Brigadier, Theo could make out the silhouette of a large cage filled with toads. Light glinted off of tiny chains and shackles around their feet.

Dorothy counted out a handful of wooden coins and handed them to Brigadier Weissbottom.

"There you go," she said. "And of course your place is always set."

"I surely am fond of your sausages, ma'am," said Brigadier Weissbottom. "I could happily eat them every day."

Dorothy laughed. "You *do* eat them every day!"

Theo pulled back from the window, shocked.

He thought about the sausages he had eaten for dinner. *Toad meat?* It made a certain amount of sense, thought Theo with dismay. Even if you could get a cow onto that gondola, Kook Bog was no place for livestock. It was no surprise that options for meat were limited. Still, toad didn't seem right.

Not that those sausages hadn't been tasty. Theo tried to put them out of his mind.

"You better keep your head down around here," Theo said to Buford.

Brigadier Weissbottom's footsteps faded along the walkway from the inn.

Chapter 17
The Bug Field Engineer

THE SUN ROSE OVER the bug fields of Kook Bog. The trees were sparser here than in the village and it was much brighter.

The bug fields were not really fields at all. Rather, they were expanses of deep, mossy mud and lush, low flora. The grass was so thick in some places it looked as though a rabbit could run across it, but the ground beneath was liquid; any rabbit that tried would sink like a stone. A green mist of aphids hung in the air like a flimsy silk scarf, and various insects fluttered and swarmed in clumps and clouds throughout the fields.

A makeshift lean-to of leaves and branches sat atop a large knot at the base of an enormous tree in the midst of the bug fields. The leaves shuddered and parted and Rudy Promovendis emerged.

It was clear that he had been roughing it. His hair, always disheveled, was now such a tangled, matted mess that it was impossible to tell where his own hair ended and the twigs and leaves began. His clothes, face, and hands were stained and caked with mud. Nevertheless, his movements were energetic and alert. A pair of primitive snowshoe-like platforms made of leaves and branches were tied to his feet. He stepped lightly off the tree and onto the mud.

Rudy tramped across the bug fields slowly but steadily in his crude mud-shoes. He carried a palette made from a chunk of tree bark.

He approached a low, thick plant with large, succulent leaves. He stripped off a piece of one leaf and squeezed it over a corner of the palette. A cloudy, greenish fluid oozed out. He touched the fluid with his pinky and tasted it. He nodded approvingly to himself.

He approached a different plant. This one had huge white and orange flowers that grew in clusters at the end of long, rough stalks. He reached into one of the flowers and plucked its pistil.

The tip of the pistil was covered with fine yellow powder. He dipped it into the greenish fluid on his palette and mixed it around. The powder swirled into the fluid.

A multifarious cloud of insects began to form around Rudy. They swirled gently around the palette.

Rudy peeled a large, white petal from the flower of still another plant. He sniffed it. He dipped a sharpened twig into the yellow-green fluid on the palette. With the twig, he drew a line on the surface of the white petal.

From the swirling cloud of bugs a column shot up in a straight trajectory at about a 45 degree angle to the ground. Rudy drew another line at a right angle to the first line. The stream of bugs turned abruptly in the air. Rudy smiled.

He reached into his pouch and withdrew his fingertip covered with white powder. With his finger, he mixed the white powder into half of the fluid on the palette. He dipped the twig into the new mix.

He drew a series of lines extending from the first two lines. In the sky above, a phalanx of purple and gold butterflies split off from the main stream of insects, fol-lowing the new lines.

Rudy mixed more ingredients and drew more lines and various insects responded in different ways. The lines he drew curled and looped on the broad white petal. He looked up and smiled.

The sky was covered with a brightly colored, complex lace of insects. The air itself seemed to shine and swirl in ornate, colorful patterns. An enormous, fleeting rainbow glistened off a column of bluebottles that extended high into the sky. Rudy scribbled some more and a red thread of ladybugs snaked crazily through a paisley pattern of pale blue moths. The sky was a bright, shifting canvas and Rudy painted his designs like an excited child.

Chapter 18
Further Into the Muck

MAYOR DIGNIGGLEBY SAT IN HIS STUDY gazing miserably at the shriveling balloon poodle.

"Daddy, we need to get Bea back," came Valerie's voice from behind him. She hadn't knocked. Digniggleby turned around in his swivel chair.

The pain on her face broke his heart.

"I can't," said Digniggleby.

"Of course you can! We have to!" insisted Valerie.

"No," said Digniggleby.

"I'm a fool. I'm no match for him."

Valerie's lip trembled.

"You can stand up to him!" she said. "You can do it for me!"

"I-I wish I could, sweetheart," said Digniggleby. "But the truth is, without him I'm nothing. All of this, everything we have, he could take it away in a moment. I have nothing to offer without him."

Digniggleby looked away from his daughter. He couldn't bear to see the tears welling up in her eyes.

"I can't go against him," he said. "I'm sorry."

Valerie stood in the doorway for a few seconds, then turned abruptly and left without a word. He could hear her muffled sobs as she ran down the hall.

Theo ate his breakfast with somewhat less gusto than he had eaten dinner the night before. The smell of the sausages was tempting, but he felt he should resist out of solidarity with Buford. Besides, he reminded himself, it was *toad*.

The inn was quiet and sunlight filtered through the trees and into the window. The old man from the night before snoozed in the corner. The clip of his headgear held the dead butt of a cigar. Dorothy looked at Theo sadly.

"It breaks my heart," she said. "Think of all life has to offer. Think of all *you* have to offer."

"I'm not offering anything," said Theo. "I don't see anybody offering to help me get out of here, either. All anybody cares about around here are convenient gizmos. Clockwork doorstops." Theo gestured at a contraption of chutes and pulleys located over the stove. "Do you need that to fry an egg?"

"It takes a lot of the guesswork out of it," said Dorothy.

"Well I don't care about that stuff," said Theo. "Practical shmactical."

The old man opened one eye.

"I know where I've heard that kind of talk before," he said. "The hermit used to talk like that. Back when he talked to people at all. If you're wondering where that kind of thinking leads, it's not pretty. Last I heard, the old kook wouldn't even use a fork and a knife."

"You didn't need to bring him up, Harry," said Dorothy.

"Who's that?" said Theo.

"What can it hurt?" said Harry. "Sounds like a kindred spirit. No sense delaying your destiny, boy. May as well get yourself fitted for a loincloth and skedaddle."

"What's he talking about?" said Theo to Dorothy.

"The hermit is just a crazy old fool who doesn't understand Kook Bog," said Dorothy. "He's the last person you ought to emulate, believe me."

"Ha!" exclaimed the Harry. "Doesn't understand indeed. Nobody understands Kook Bog better! He knows everything there is to know about this place and he understands just fine. He *rejects* it is all. That's what stings. They say the only reason he's still here is that he rejects Mossville even more."

"You mean he knows how to get out?" said Theo.

"So they say," said Harry. "It doesn't matter though. He won't help you. He doesn't help anybody."

"Tell me how to find him," said Theo.

"Why would I do that?" said Harry.

"Why indeed!" said Dorothy. "The last thing a boy your age needs is to be traipsing around the wilderness around here."

"He can traipse all he wants, for all I care," said Harry. "He doesn't need my help for that."

"What if I found a way to get out of Kook Bog?" said Theo. "Don't you want that?"

"Hmm," said Harry. He fished a fresh cigar out of his pocket and replaced the butt on the clip of his headgear. He turned a key to wind a spring mechanism, and the various parts of the contraption clicked into motion. A lighter flicked and extended to light the cigarette and the bellows opened to suck air through the cigar. With a little hiss a cloud of smoke burst into his face. "Not especially."

"Well, I bet a lot of people around here do," said Theo. "You could do it for them, if you're so eager to help people."

"I'll tell you what," said Harry. "I'll make you a deal. I'll tell you how to find the hermit. Ballpark, that is. Nobody knows exactly where he is from time time to time, but I can tell you how to get to where he's been seen. If you manage to get yourself out of Kook Bog, then that'll be the end of it. But if you *don't*, then you pay me."

"Harry…," said Dorothy in warning tone. But she only shook her head.

"I don't have anything to pay you with," said Theo.

"Oh, yes you do," said Harry. He looked at the lump in Theo's shirt pocket.

Buford squirmed uneasily.

"I love the sausages," said Harry. "But it sure has been a long time since I had a nice fillet all to myself."

It scarcely crossed his mind that he might be sacrificing Buford by agreeing. *Of course* he would get out of Kook Bog, he thought. He was impatient, irritated, and impulsive. He agreed to Harry's conditions immediately.

An hour later he stood at the neglected edge of the village where decks and walkways ended. Some of the walkways were partially sunken into the mud. Some had missing boards and planks so rotten they gave way like wet bread. Theo took a piece of old lumber from a broken handrail and extended it into the mud. He felt around for a shallow patch. He stepped off the walk-way and waist deep into the bog.

The going was exhausting. It was slow enough having to wade through the mud which sometimes came as high as his neck. Worse still was the winding, haphazard route he needed to follow to stay in shallow mud and keep his head above the sur-face. He got as far away from the village as he could before he stopped to rest. He pulled himself up on to a broad, flat rock. He looked back at the village. He'd made it further than he thought. In the distance ahead loomed the great black ridge that separated Kook Bog from Mossville. He could hear the muffled roar of the mud river at its base. Sitting on the rock he contemplated the deal he'd made. There was no doubt he needed to look for his father and to rescue Bea. To do those things he was determined to es-cape from Kook Bog. When the old man made his offer he'd jumped at the chance. But now, with some time to think in the middle of this oozing, burbling wilderness, he feared he had mis-taken his own determination for certainty. There was no guarantee he would find the hermit, and even if he did there was no guaran-tee he'd be able to convince the hermit to help him.

Buford squirmed in Theo's pocket.

"I'm not going to let anything happen to you," said Theo. "We're going to get out of here."

He only wished he could convince himself.

Gnats and flies swarmed around the rag on his arm, attracted to the dried-up stains of leonore extract. Theo waved them away.

He withdrew a tightly folded piece of paper from inside his belt. He unfolded it and studied the crudely inked map. He looked around himself to try to identify landmarks drawn on the map. He frowned. The old man had given him chicken scratches. Was the scribble in the corner supposed to be the copse of trees to his right or the cluster of reeds to the left?

Overhead, dark clouds threatened.

After altogether too much guesswork with the map, Theo eventually made it to a broad expanse of rushing mud dotted by rocks. He could make out the words "rock field" on the part of the map corresponding to where he thought he was. So far so good.

The clouds had made good on their threats, and a steady rain had been gaining in strength for nearly an hour. The rocks were slippery and mud rushed in knotty rivulets between them.

The rocks varied in size and in the distance between them. Some were no more than an easy step away. Others required an effort to leap and some luck to avoid slipping into the rushing mud below and breaking his neck.

The rocks became sparser ahead as the mud deepened to become a wide, fast river. Far away in the hazy distance up the river, Theo could make out the enormous black base of the Kook Bog end of the Suction-Flux Hydro-Debogilator.

To Theo's right and left the rocks were still near enough to each other to continue. He would have to follow the banks either upstream or downstream.

Theo consulted the map, but it was so wet and smeared as to be completely unreadable. Theo could make out the rough shape of an arrow drawn along the bank of the river, but the ink had soaked clear through the paper. He couldn't tell which side of the map was the front. He turned the paper and over, trying to ascertain which direction the arrow pointed. What once had been words were now just cloudy patches of ink. The soaked paper disintegrated to pulp in his fingers.

There was nothing left to do but take his chances. Theo took a long step over to the nearest rock to his right, upstream.

At that moment, Buford leaped from Theo's pocket and landed smack in the middle of the rock Theo had just left.

"What are you doing?" cried Theo.

Buford leaped again in the opposite direction. He landed on the next rock in the downstream direction. He turned around and looked up at Theo.

Buford seemed determined to follow the banks downstream. Theo shrugged. The map had crumbled to nothing in the heavy rain and he had no idea where to go now. The toad's instincts couldn't be any worse than his own. He stepped back onto the downstream rock and followed Buford.

Buford leaped again, and again Theo stepped to follow him. But this time his foot did not land as it should. He had not seen the dark patch of wet moss on the rock. Before he knew what had happened he had tumbled head over heels straight into the rushing flood of mud.

Chapter 19
The Patent Administrator's Troubling Ward

MR. CESS'S MANSION WAS WELL equipped for experimental and constructive pursuits of all varieties. Among its many rooms were fully-stocked metallurgy, woodworking and glassblowing studios. Cess could modestly boast a hard-won level of competence in all of these disciplines. He had honed his skills through years of building other people's inventions. Lazy he was not.

Mr. Cess's experimental laboratory was located down a spiral staircase in the corner of his office. The laboratory was stocked with shelves upon shelves of chemicals. It had faucets and nozzles for water, oxygen, hydrogen, helium, liquid nitrogen and sulfuric acid. A wide selection of other gasses and liquids were available in pressurized canisters. Metal cupboards and drawers overflowed with wires, electrodes, pith balls, heavy-duty batteries, and electromagnetic coils. Hooks on the wall held every kind of tool imaginable, from hacksaws to circuit testers. Cess's beloved slide-rule, the very one that had saved his young life, hung in a special place beside his framed Certificate of Commendation for Exceptional Scientific Genius from the mayor.

A very special tray of pollens, plant extracts, and insect secretions was arranged next to the broad metal workbench. Upon the workbench, motionless but for the occasional twitch, lay Bea.

Cess studied the plans for the harvester's bug drive. He wore a white lab coat and held a beaker full of red-orange fluid. Ballhatchet and Dooley stood at attention. They wore blue-green scrubs.

"This should liven things up a bit," muttered Cess, inserting an eyedropper into the beaker and filling it with the fluid.

Ballhatchet and Dooley watched Cess bend forward to administer the fluid. For a moment, Bea did not react.

Suddenly, a cloud of gnats emerged from the sides of Bea's head and the fireflies in her eyes flickered and twitched.

"This doesn't seem quite right," said Cess to himself. Then louder, he said, "Ballhatchet! Dandelion!"

"Which was the dandelion again?" said Ballhatchet.

"The yellow one, you idiot!" hissed Dooley.

"Whitish!" said Cess.

"Ah! Got it," said Ballhatchet. He handed Cess an eyedropper filled with whitish fluid. "I still don't see how this doll is like a harvester."

Shut up, Ballhatchet," said Dooley. "Mr. Cess is trying to concentrate!"

"What, I'm not bothering him," said Ballhatchet. "Am I bothering you, Mr. Cess?"

Cess rolled his eyes and applied the whitish fluid.

Suddenly, Bea sat bolt upright. The bugs buzzed loudly and circulated in full force. Their motion was rapid and they flowed in tight formation over Bea's whole body. Bea reached towards the tray of pollens and extracts. Ballhatchet pulled the tray away.

"Whoa there! That's not for you!"

Bea leaped off the table and began grabbing at everything she could. Cess raced ahead of her to protect the rows of beakers on the counter.

"Now, just a moment!" he said. "Hold on there!"

But Bea was off and running. She ran under the table. Her bugs shrieked. Ballhatchet dove to grab her but missed, crashing into a closet full of beakers and tubes. Bea shot straight into the air, launched like a ball from a cannon of bugs. She bounced like rubber from the ceiling and somersaulted the ground. The insects made a chattering, clucking sound.

"She's laughing!" said Ballhatchet, pulling himself to his feet.

Indeed, Bea seemed to be enjoying herself. She ran in circles and shook her arms and head. She grabbed a cable attached to a large oscilloscope and shook it. The oscilloscope toppled to the ground with a crash and its cathode ray tube exploded in a burst of flame. Everyone froze and stared at the mess, including Bea. She broke into sobbing movements and the buzzing of her insects became a piercing wail.

"Oh dear," said Cess.

It was Dooley's idea to duct tape her to the table. With great effort they managed to secure her to the table in a mad cocoon of tape, but this only made the insects more agitated. Though Bea's limbs were pinned, the movement of the bugs made it seem she was flailing more wildly than ever. A burst of gnats struck Dooley full in the face with the force of a fist. A moth the size of robin's egg pelted Ballhatchet smack in the eye.

"Ow!" cried Ballhatchet.

Cess scrambled to get the tray of pollens and extracts into some kind of order. Powders and liquids were spilled all over the tray and mingled haphazardly. A thin wisp of greenish smoke rose from the tray. In a panic, Cess took off his white lab coat and tried to extinguish whatever was emitting the smoke, but this only succeeded in mingling the chemicals further. He gave up. He dove under the table and cowered under the workbench as the room filled with a furious, chaotic hurricane of bugs. Ballhatchet and Dooley followed soon after. The three of them huddled together under the metal table, hoping for the banging above to subside.

"Blast!" said Cess.

"I didn't think it looked much like a harvester," said Ballhatchet. "I think you might have the manuals mixed up."

Cess seethed silently.

"That kid seemed pretty handy with it," said Ballhatchet.

"Ballhatchet, will you shut it already?" exclaimed Dooley. "Can't you see Mr. Cess is trying to think? Good grief! What I wouldn't give to have a partner who wasn't a complete idiot for a change!"

Cess pondered Dooley's comment.

"Indeed," he said.

Mayor Digniggleby sat alone in his study. From the walls, awards and accolades seemed to mock him. The *Annual Mossville Award For Outstanding Contributions to the Municipal Benefit*, photographs of himself being flattered by dignitaries, ribbons and certificates too numerous to mention in honor of the Suction-Flux Hydro-Debogilator. His eyes fell on the framed photograph of his inauguration day, propped up on the desk. He reached over and placed it face down.

That wasn't enough. He took the picture in his hands. He stood up and collected the memorabilia from the walls, the desk, and the shelves of the study. He pulled an old trunk out of the corner, opened it and dumped everything in.

At the bottom of the trunk a yellowed piece of paper caught his eye. He dug down and picked it up.

On the paper was a simple drawing of an oval. It was the very one that he had presented at the patent office that fateful day so long ago. Digniggleby looked at the paper for a long, long time.

Cess sat alone in the darkness of his office. His face was welted and bug-bitten. The sound of buzzing and rattling in the laboratory below was muffled through the floor.

On the desk in front of him stood a large magnetic tape editor made of Bakelite and bronze. From either side of the editor extended a metal arm holding a reel. Between the reels and through the tape-head at the base of the editor ran a length of audio tape. A curled, tuba-shaped speaker extended from the middle part of the editor. Cess pushed a little lever right and left to wind the audio tape forward and back. He skipped from snippet to snippet as the tinny sound of Rudy Promovendis's voice emerged amid the hiss from the speaker: *...I'm going to change the world...You leave my son out...he is not involved in my work...if you're trying to steal my inventi...*

Cess smiled to himself. He pressed down on the editor's blade and cut the tape.

Chapter 20
A Fruitless Consultation and an
Unexpected Reprieve

THEO OPENED HIS EYES to find himself lying on his back on a broad, warm rock in the sun. His clothes were caked with mud. He put his hands to his face to find that his face had been wiped clean.

Buford sat on his chest.

Theo set Buford aside and sat up. He patted himself all over to check for injuries. Aside from some bruises he seemed to be in one piece. Beside the rock, the wide river of mud raged. At the far side of the river the black, craggy ridge rose abruptly.

As the far end of the rocks, about a ten yards away from where Theo sat, stood a rudimentary teepee made of three large, leafy tree branches. Theo stood and walked toward the teepee.

From the far side of the teepee Theo heard a munching sound. He peeked cautiously around the teepee.

The hermit sat cross-legged on the rock, naked except for a dingy old pair of plaid shorts. His body was just leathery skin and bones and his eyes were sunken. His white hair stuck out straight from his head in clumps several feet long and his beard extended to his belly. He chewed on something crunchy. In front of him was a large pile of dead cicadas.

Theo approached the hermit.

"Thanks," said Theo.

The hermit didn't look up. "For what?"

"For pulling me out," said Theo.

The hermit shrugged.

"Wasn't me," he said.

Theo looked around. There was no trace of anyone else.

"Well, who was it then?" said Theo.

"I dunno," said the hermit. "A bird maybe. Maybe a chip-munk. You don't look like you weigh much."

Theo wasn't sure if the hermit was making a joke, but he didn't find it very funny.

"I need to get out of Kook Bog," he said.

The hermit munched silently for a while without responding. At length, he picked up a cicada from his pile and extended his hand to Theo.

"Cicada?" he said.

Theo crinkled his nose.

"Did you hear me?" he said. "I want you to tell me how to get out of here."

The hermit looked at Buford, who sat a few feet away.

"I bet you want one," said the hermit. He flicked the cicada at Buford. Buford's tongue shot out and snapped up the insect.

The hermit turned back to Theo. He gestured at the looming, precipitous ridge across the wide, wild river of mud.

"Thataway," he said.

"I can't get across that," said Theo. "I need to know another way."

The hermit scoffed and took a bite of a cicada.

"You ought to try one," he said. "They're tastier than they look. You won't appreciate the subtleties, of course, but you don't need to be a connoisseur to enjoy 'em."

"I don't want to eat your stupid bugs," said Theo. "I want to get out of here."

The hermit shot Theo an irritated look.

"All right then," he said. "Get out of here. Let me eat my lunch in peace."

"They say you know how to get out of Kook Bog," said Theo. "The real way."

The hermit scrunched up his face.

"Maybe I do. But I'd be wasting my breath telling you," said the hermit.

Theo fumed.

"Those kooks were right about you," he said. "You're no help to anybody."

For a second, a hurt look flashed across the hermit's eyes. But a moment later it was gone.

"Me and the world are even-Steven, boy," the hermit.

The hermit flicked a cicada straight at Theo's face.

"One for the road," said the hermit.

Theo flinched. Buford's tongue flashed and the cicada vanished. Buford croaked contentedly.

Theo stood for a moment on the verge of tears. There was nothing more he could say. The old man at the inn had been right. The hermit was no use to anyone. Theo walked back to the far edge of the rock. Far in the distance, he could see the curling smoke from the village chimneys. He turned back to look once more at the hermit's teepee. He could hear the hermit still munching away.

Theo gulped down his disappointment and stepped into the mud.

Berke sat on his stool on the dock at the gondola terminus. His 15-foot-range Remote Person Extractor leaned against his shoulder, looking suspiciously like an ordinary stick.

The gondola clanked and Berke jolted awake, but there was no splash. Nobody was aboard the gondola.

Berke squinted at the gondola, puzzled. There was something else there. A length of heavy rope hung from the bar of the gondola. At the end of the rope, about a foot short of the mud, dangled a loop in the shape of a hangman's noose.

Berke reached out with the Remote Person Extractor (which really was an incredibly useful and multi-purpose device) and fished the loop over to the dock.

A small white envelope was affixed with cellophane tape to the end of the loop. Across the front of the envelope, in crisp, handwritten script, were the words *To Whom It May Concern*.

Theo trudged through the mud towards the village, swatting at the bugs that still clustered around his arm. His stomach rumbled. He wasn't hungry enough to start eating cicadas, but he was getting close. He thought about Dorothy's sausages and a wave of guilt came over him.

He'd lost the wager. The old man was going to demand his payment. And what would Theo do then? He tried to think of a plan. He could refuse to turn Buford over to the old man. But Dorothy had been a witness to his promise. Everyone in Kook Bog would know he was not to be trusted. If he was going to be stuck here that didn't seem like a good way to begin. Besides, it wouldn't take many of them ganging up on him to take Buford by force, and then he wouldn't even have his toad for a friend.

He could let Buford go and tell the old man that Buford escaped. Who knew what the old man would demand as a substitute payment, but surely it would be better than betraying Buford. Of course that assumed Buford would go if Theo let him. Thus far, Buford had proved to be a stubbornly loyal companion.

Theo's stomach knotted up. He couldn't simply turn Buford over to be filleted. He was far too hungry himself to consider making a dash into the wilderness. But if he put up a fight it was doubtful Dorothy would extend her hospitality to him any further.

He felt Buford squirm in his pocket.

"I'll think of something," he said.

He'd have to buy some time until he got something to eat. He would sneak to the inn and ask Dorothy for a meal first. If he was lucky, maybe the old man wouldn't be there. After that, who knew. Maybe he'd fight. Maybe he'd run off into the bog again and never come back. If he could only get some food in his belly maybe it would be easier to come up with a plan.

The sun was setting as the edge of the village came into view. He could see the lights through the trees. There were the broken railings and the crumbling walkways of the neglected edge of the village he had departed from the day before.

But it wasn't neglected now.

On the contrary, there were people, *many* people, congregated on the deck. And not just one deck, either. More people gathered even as he approached. The entire edge of the village, the decks, the boardwalks and the broken, disused communication gazebo were all filling with people. The whole of Kook Bog seemed to be gathering here at the village edge. And as Theo waded closer, he became uncomfortably aware that they were all looking at him.

So much for sneaking in for some grub.

It was much worse than he had imagined. He would never have thought the old man would go to such lengths for a toad. And he certainly never would have dreamed the entire village of Kook Bog would have acted in such solidarity to enforce the deal.

His heart sank. He couldn't possibly fight the whole village. They'd tear him limb from limb.

Theo stopped about a hundred yards from the deck. He looked around for alternatives. There was nowhere else to go, only trees and mud in every direction. Hunger gnawed at his belly.

A stout tree stood ahead of him just to the left. He veered slightly in that direction so that his body was partially concealed from the view of the villagers. As quickly as he could, he pulled Buford out of his pocket with his hidden hand and tossed the toad away.

"Go!" he whispered out of the corner of his mouth without a sidelong glance. He waded straight towards the village.

The decks groaned under the weight of the villagers who had gathered to watch Theo as he returned. He pushed his way through the last of the mud and stood at the edge of the crumbling deck. The crowd of villagers backed away from the edge, giving him space to climb onto the deck.

He stood up and looked around. All eyes were on him. The expressions on people's faces were unreadable. The old man was there too, staring at Theo just like everyone else.

Theo started to explain that Buford had escaped, but no sooner had he opened his mouth than he heard a thump on the deck beside his feet. He looked down to see Buford, sitting attentively at his side. With a start, he reached down and picked the toad up. He held Buford defensively in both hands against his chest. His heart pounded.

From the midst of the crowd, Berke lumbered forward. He stood in front of Theo with a look of stunned disbelief.

"I'm not quite sure how to explain this," he said. "I think I'd better just show you."

He unfolded a piece of paper and held it out for Theo to read. On it was a hastily handwritten note. It read:

Send the boy back up.

Regards,
Cess

Chapter 21
The Dawn of a New Era in Labor-Saving Automata

AFTER A HEARTY MEAL of potatoes, cabbage, and mushrooms, Theo sat in the loop of rope dangling below the gondola, his feet submerged in the mud.

"I haven't really done this before," said Berke. "I assume it's set not to shake so much on the way up this time, but you probably want to hold tight just in case."

Theo held tight to the rope and Berke pulled a lever on the dock. With a jolt, the gondola began to rise smoothly.

The crowd of villagers watched Theo go.

Suddenly, Buford the Toad—for reasons apparent only within his own amphibian cerebrum—leaped out of Theo's shirt pocket and onto the deck.

"Buford!" cried Theo, swinging his arms vainly to try to catch the toad and just barely keeping his balance.

Berke looked around his feet for the source of the thump, but Buford was already gone. He hopped away between legs and dove under a walkway before anyone even knew he was there.

Mr. Cess spoke gently, like a kindhearted uncle.

"I was hasty in my judgment of you, my boy," he said. "As Chief Patent Administrator, it is my responsibility to ensure that such an extraordinary creation is properly cared for. I see now that you are up to that task."

Bea lay quietly on the metal workbench.

Theo was still disoriented from the unprecedented reverse gondola ride. At any rate, he thought, Mr. Cess had reunited him with Bea, and that was a good thing. Perhaps all the trouble so far had just been a misunderstanding. Theo hoped so.

"That Diniggleby girl, though," continued Cess. "Clearly unfit. To treat such a delicate creation like an old rag doll! You saw its condition when you arrived. It was a grave failure of judgment on your part to entrust it to such a frivolous child."

Theo frowned. What had Valerie done? He had counted on her. Clearly, she had let him down and nearly cost Bea her life.

"It was a good thing I stepped in when I did, or our precious creature would most surely have been…," began Cess. "No, perish the thought. You've learned your lesson, and I forgive you for the lapse."

Theo was not sure what he had done to require Mr. Cess's forgiveness, but he did not see how it could serve him to argue. He said nothing.

Mr. Cess's voice dripped with compassion.

"You know she needs you," he said.

Theo looked at Bea and nodded. This much was certainly true.

"I know," he said.

It was a relief to hear Mr. Cess say it. But there was still something else on Theo's mind. He had to ask. He took a deep breath.

"Do you know where my dad is?" said Theo.

Mr. Cess sighed deeply.

"I think you'd better come with me," he said.

Mr. Cess led Theo up the spiral staircase to his office and gestured for him to sit down.

"Family is so important," said Mr. Cess, seemingly overcome with sadness. "And betrayal… Betrayal by a parent is a pain no child should ever have to suffer."

Theo squinched his face in bewilderment. He had no idea what Mr. Cess could be talking about. Mr. Cess's voice trembled and his eyes welled with tears.

"Which is why it saddens me beyond words," said Cess, "to be the bearer of what I'm sure will be devastating news."

Mr. Cess strode over to the reel-to-reel tape player on his desk.

144

"Your father came to me several days ago," said Mr. Cess. "He was concerned about the security of his intellectual property."

Mr. Cess held his finger over the play lever of the tape player.

"To be honest," said Mr. Cess. "I don't think he was himself. He was raving. You mustn't hold his words against him."

"What? What did he say?" Theo made no effort to hide his confusion.

Mr. Cess pressed the lever. A hissing sound emanated from the speaker, broken by occasional clicks and silences. Then came Rudy's voice, tinny but unmistakeable: "*I'm going to leave my son. He's trying to steal my work!*"

Mr. Cess flicked the lever again quickly to stop the playback. "I'm so, so sorry, my boy."

Theo was gobsmacked. It made no sense. Him? Steal his own father's work? How could his father have even conceived of such a... Theo paused. His mind raced. Of course, he had done that very thing. He knew he had been forbidden to dabble with his father's chemicals and bug-control methods. Yet he had gone ahead and done it anyway in secret. But... hadn't his father only been concerned for Theo's safety? He couldn't really have considered his own son a *threat*?

"This doesn't make any sense," Theo barely managed to whisper.

"Indeed, what could be more senseless than a man's abandonment of his own flesh and blood," said Mr. Cess. "The very fruit of his loins."

Theo was speechless. Mr. Cess stood back and rocked lightly on his heels, letting it all sink in.

"Alas and alack," said Mr. Cess at last, his tone turning suddenly matter-of-fact. "Senseless things happen. We have to buck up."

Theo was too confused to answer.

"It is time to think about the future, my boy," said Mr. Cess. "Think about, what did you say its name was..."

"Bea," said Theo.

"Yes, Bea. Think about that," said Mr. Cess. "I will see to it that you have all the resources you need to help it. But not only that. No-one deserves to be alone, and that marvelous creature is no exception. I want to help you use your gifts to create more like it. Imagine, a whole family of wonderful, gentle creatures just like it as companions! All of them needing you, loving you. So grateful to *you* for bringing them into existence. What a happy, happy scene! You'll forget all about that deadbeat old man of yours."

Theo sat quietly, considering Mr. Cess's words.

"I do think Bea would like some friends," he said.

"Son, you just tell me what you need," said Mr. Cess.

Shoppers bustled from shop to shop in the center of Mossville. A red-cheeked, curly-haired little girl waited in front of a cheese shop as her mother stood in the queue with her arms full of Brie. The little girl cradled a pajama-clad baby doll nearly as big as herself. She looked up to see Ballhatchet and Dooley standing in front of her. Her big, brown eyes widened.

"Official patent office business," said Dooley, holding open the mouth of a large canvas bag. "I'm afraid we're going to have to take this."

Ballhatchet snatched the baby doll out of the girl's hands. In a single swift motion, he popped the doll's head off and tossed it into the canvas bag. He handed the headless doll back to the girl, who shrieked and burst into hysterical tears, then ran into the cheese shop.

"Kids today are awful materialistic," said Ballhatchet as the two of them walked off down the street. "Somebody needs to tell them happiness isn't about having toys."

"What do you reckon happiness is about, Ballhatchet?" asked Dooley. "For the sake of conversation."

Ballhatchet pondered.

"I guess it's about having a sense of self-worth and personal fulfillment in what you do," said Ballhatchet. "That'd be my answer."

They stopped at *M.Routin's Finer Baubles and Playthings for Today's Well-Mannered Child* and walked straight to the counter.

"We'll take the lot," said Dooley, gesturing broadly at the doll section of the shop.

"The lot?" said the slim, bespectacled clerk.

"And we'll need a seventy-five percent discount, since we're only going to use the heads."

"Why, that's not possible!" cried the clerk.

Ballhatchet leaned threateningly over the clerk and growled.

"Official patent office business," said Dooley. "Let's keep this orderly."

A few minutes later, Ballhatchet and Dooley emerged from the shop laden with gigantic sacks full of doll heads over their shoulders.

The laboratory window was wide open and clouds of bugs moved freely in and out. They swarmed and eddied outside the window. Rows of mechanical bodies were laid out in various states of disassembly. Unused parts of Rudy's harvester were strewn about, other parts had been reconstituted as parts of the automatons. A heap of doll heads filled a one corner of the laboratory.

Theo went from one automaton to the next, screwing on heads, assembling parts, and administering chemicals. Bugs swirled in the window and responded to his concoctions.

Bea followed Theo closely, peeking out from behind his leg at her numerous imitators. She flinched whenever one of them moved.

Mr. Cess also followed, watching intently over Theo's shoulder. He scratched notes in his note pad.

"Ah, I see. Fascinating... Yes, yes. Extraordinary. The leonore and the rose powder... And that there is aphid honeydew I take it?"

"That holds them to the patterns," said Theo. "It keeps the programs running smoothly."

"Indeed!" said Mr. Cess, scribbling eagerly into his notebook. "It won't be long now, will it!"

They moved along to another part of the laboratory, where a group of automatons passed a bright red ball among themselves. Theo spritzed some fluid into the air and the group passed the ball faster and more precisely.

Theo turned to Bea, cowering behind his leg.

"Go on, Bea," he said.

"Join them. They're your friends."

Bea shook her head.

"She's shy," said Theo to Cess.

Mr. Cess smiled stiffly and wrote in his notebook.

The patent office murmured with the rustle of paper and the muted buzz of administrative chatter, punctuated by the occasional bang of a rubber stamp. At the ding of the elevator the room went silent. The door opened and Cess stepped out. He was accompanied by Theo and Bea, who hugged Theo's leg tightly. The elevator shut behind them.

"Ladies and gentlemen!" boomed Cess. "I have an announcement to make!"

The clerks held their breath.

"As you all know," said Cess, "I have toiled ceaselessly for years at the service of the betterment of mankind. And for all of those years, you all have worked under me, attempting, in your own meager ways, to help me in my efforts."

Theo looked out across the vast office space. The clerks sat bolt upright in their desks, so still they looked almost unreal.

"And yet," continued Cess, "for all those years, nothing approaching the extraordinary creation that I am about to show you has ever appeared. Not until this lad here came along."

Theo attempted a smile. He was happy about the praise, but the reception wasn't very warm. In fact, nobody moved a muscle.

"The truth is, this young, fresh-faced boy has more genius under his *fingernails* than the lot of you combined."

Theo's smile faded. This wasn't quite the wording he'd have chosen. He was glad to see that the clerks still showed no response.

"Which is of course why he is now my second in command, and you are all still a bunch of dead-end ground-floor clerks. But at least that much is about to change. No longer will you toil without reward or recognition in this dismal little office!"

The elevator dinged again and the door opened. A dozen baby doll-headed automatons stepped out amid the noisy buzz of insects. The automatons each wore a burlap potato sack for clothing.

"Ladies and gentlemen, meet your replacements," said Cess.

At this, the clerks finally reacted. The room erupted in gasps as the automatons marched to their desks. The elevator rose again to collect another batch.

A young clerk piped up. "But Mr. Cess, what are *we* going to do?"

"Why, enjoy the autumn of your life, of course," said Cess.

"But, I'm only twenty!" said the clerk.

"Well then, I would hunker down for a long winter if I were you," said Cess. "Now off you go! Don't crowd the exits!"

Ballhatchet and Dooley wandered through the crowded city center, collecting heads from any child they saw with a doll. Ballhatchet carried the bag. Dooley grabbed a bundle from a little boy, but it turned out to be a dog and yelped, giving Dooley a fright.

A notice plastered on a light post caught Ballhatchet's eye. It read:

PUBLIC ANNOUNCEMENT BY THE MAYOR

Tuesday Afternoon
Main Town Square

"What's this all about?" said Ballhatchet.

"You got me," said Dooley.

Ballhatchet and Dooley looked at each other. It was the kind of thing Mr. Cess would want to be apprised of before it happened, rather than after.

"We'd better head back," said Dooley.

Chapter 22
A Well-Intentioned Confession and a
Forceful Response

A CROWD HAD GATHERED around the platform in the town square. Constable Fleabo and Deputy Deepak stood at either corner of the front of the platform. Mayor Diniggleby made his way through the crowd to the platform, accompanied by Cynthia and Valerie.

"Meriweather, what are you planning to say?" whispered Cynthia. "I demand that you tell me!"

"Trust me, Cynthia," said Diniggleby. "It has to be this way."

"What's he doing?" asked Valerie to her mother.

"I don't know, honey," said Cynthia.

Mayor Diniggleby climbed the steps to the platform.

"You two wait here. I have to do this myself," he said.

Mayor Diniggleby stood in the middle of the stage and adjusted the microphone stand to his height. He tapped loudly on the microphone and cleared his throat.

"Ladies and gentlemen," he said. "There is a matter that has weighed heavily on my heart. I have a terrible confession to make." He sniffled and scrunched up his face, then composed himself and continued, "I am not who you think I am."

A murmur rose from the crowd. Valerie and Cynthia looked at each other nervously.

"That is to say, I *am* who you think I am. But... I haven't done what you think I've done," Diniggleby stammered. He took a deep breath. "I did not invent the Suction-Flux Hydro Debogilator."

A gasp rose from the crowd. Cynthia's mouth moved silently, as if it were searching for the words to explain what she had just heard. Valerie wrinkled her brow deeply.

"The only thing I ever invented was this," said Digniggleby. He held the drawing of an oval up humbly with both hands before his chest. "It's a paperweight. It's oblong. It's, uh, made of soap."

The murmuring of the crowd increased.

"I humbly submit it to you," said Digniggleby. "But I do understand if you don't feel it's enough to warrant my continued service as your mayor."

Suddenly, Cess's voice boomed out from the back of the crowd.

"Outrageous!" thundered Cess as he strode through the crowd towards the stage, his little entourage in tow. Theo walked alongside Cess, jogging every few steps to keep up, and Bea ran alongside Theo.

"Oh, Mr. Cess," sputtered Digniggleby. "I'm sorry. I simply can't—"

A group of automatons had already mounted the stage. Before Digniggleby could finish his sentence they flung a canvas sack over his head, muffling his words.

Cess flew up the steps to the stage.

"I think we have heard quite enough!" he spoke into the microphone. "As Chief Patent Administrator and second in line to the mayorship of Mossville I hereby declare a state of emergency! Constable Fleabo, please stand by in case my men require your assistance!"

The automatons descended on Cynthia and Valerie with canvas sacks.

"Goodness!" exclaimed Cynthia. "Stop it!"

"Get away from me!" shouted Valerie. She looked at Theo. "Don't do this!"

Theo turned his face away from Valerie. Bea shook her head frantically. Suddenly, Bea dashed out from behind Theo and made straight for Valerie. Bea pushed one of the automatons away from Valerie, but the others quickly swarmed to its defense. They shoved Bea to the ground.

Theo rushed to pick her up. He snatched her away from the struggle.

"Easy, Bea. It's okay," he tried to calm her.

The army of automatons hoisted the three squirming canvas sacks up and began to carry them out of the town square.

Cess's voice boomed from the speakers.

"Citizens!" he said. "We have been duped! The villain has admitted to his own mendacity! But have no fear. Law and order shall be restored to Mossville! Justice shall be done!"

The army of automatons marched in formation throughout the city of Mossville and its environs. They burst in on the Baron LePeen as he sat on his velvet chaise longue eating strawberry shortcake. They plucked him off of his cushion and stuffed him into a canvas bag.

A river of automatons ran through the town bearing wriggling sacks full of clerks, magistrates, orphans, and pets. Cess had kept an exhaustive list over the years of everyone who had ever cheated him, insulted him, stepped in his way, or looked at him askance. It was a very long list.

A tower of automatons, each standing on the shoulders of the next, reached from the ground to the Kook Bog gondola. One by one the struggling contents of the canvas sacks were hoisted up, dumped onto the bucket, and jettisoned off to the waiting mire.

Digniggleby, Cynthia, and Valerie each got their turns on the gondola. They shot out over the sprawling periphery of Mossville, over the craggy black ridge and down into the soupy bog below.

In Kook Bog, Berke was having a busy day. One by one the Digniggglebys splashed down into the mud. One by one he fished them out with the 15-Foot Remote Person Extractor.

"Another one!" he shouted into the tin can telephone, as Valerie climbed onto the dock, covered head to toe in thick mud.

Valerie screamed up at the receding gondola. "You *jerk!*"

Baron LePeen splashed down and Berke helped him to the dock. As he did his best to wipe himself off, the gondola banged in again and a sheep splashed down into the mud.

"Oh dear," said Baron LePeen.

Berke spoke into the tin can phone.

"Looks like a sheep," he said.

Suddenly, Valerie leaped forward and grabbed the tin can phone from his hand.

"Gimme that!" she said.

"Hey!" said Berke.

Valerie pulled the phone's twine loose from its hook and flung it with all her might at the gondola as it pulled away. The can fell onto the gondola and wedged itself between the bucket and the bar of the frame. As the gondola pulled away the phone's twine pulled free from one hook after another over the Kook Bog village, until the line of twine followed the gondola straight from the switchboard gazebo in the center of the village. The gondola pulled the twine taut as it rose into the clouds.

Valerie ran along the boardwalks and decks towards the village as fast as her legs would carry her, following the twine to its origin at the switchboard gazebo.

Mr. Cess and Theo stood on the balcony near the gondola launch looking out over the center of Mossville as the regiments of baby-doll automatons marched through the town. The hum of millions of insects was deafening even from this height. The automatons advanced mercilessly through the alleys and streets. They were small, but in their numbers they were an unstoppable force. Terrified townspeople cowered before the advancing ranks. The luckiest were thrown roughly out of the way, while others were stuffed into canvas bags and hauled away.

"Extraordinary!" said Mr. Cess. "And all thanks to your brilliant creative gifts. Such an accomplishment! So many lives touched."

Theo nodded. There was no denying he felt a measure of satisfaction. He had always been an outsider in Mossville. The people of the town had always been hasty to point their fingers at him. He watched the automatons collect the fat man who had accused Theo of stealing a watch, and it was hard to suppress a smile. Who was the ragamuffin now?

Bea cowered and trembled. She no longer clung to Theo's leg. She hung back, near the far end of the balcony. Theo went to her. He bent down and spoke kindly.

"You don't need to be afraid," he said. "They're your friends. I made them for you."

Bea looked down at the chaotic scene below and shook her head.

"They have to be tough sometimes to be accepted is all," said Theo.

Cess glanced over at Bea with a sneer.

"A little jealous of the attention?" he said.

Suddenly, Valerie's voice rang out from the gondola platform.

"Theo!" she cried.

Theo looked up to see the tin can phone wedged in the gondola. Valerie's voice continued.

"If you can hear me, I just want you to know that I thought you were better than this! I thought you cared about Bea! But now I know that you just want to have control."

Theo shook his head and crinkled his nose indignantly.

"That's not true," he said, half to Bea and half to himself.

Valerie's voice continued. "That's why you made all those fakes! Those monsters aren't like Bea and you know it! Bea knows it too!"

Bea trembled violently.

"Desperate people will say anything," said Cess. He strode toward the gondola launch platform.

Theo gripped Bea by the shoulders. "She's wrong!"

Down in Kook Bog, Valerie crouched on the roof of the central communication gazebo, gripping the end of the tin can telephone in both hands. She really was desperate. She clenched her eyes and wondered what else she could say to possibly convince Theo he was making a mistake.

She felt a tap on her shoulder.

She looked up to see Rudy Promovendis standing beside her on the roof of the gazebo. He was a disheveled, mud-caked mess, but his eyes shone with energy. He smiled at Valerie and held out his hand.

"Let me talk to him," said Rudy.

Up above, on the balcony, Cess had just reached the gondola platform when Rudy's voice came through the can.

"Theo?" it said.

Theo's jaw dropped. "Dad?"

But Cess had heard all he wanted to hear. He drew a large Bowie knife from his jacket.

"Enough of this!" he said, and cut the twine in a single, swift stroke. The tin can clattered on the stairwells below and the twine drifted off in the wind.

"As a matter of fact, I've had enough of that whole blasted bog!" said Cess. "It was a fine place to toss the riffraff when I didn't have other choices. But now that we've got some order around here, there's no point doing things halfway!"

Cess strode into his office.

"What are you doing?" said Theo.

"Kook Bog is more trouble than it's worth!" boomed Cess.

Theo looked out over the violence below. A gang of automa-tons pummeled an old man, another group threw a golden re-triever into a sack, and still others hoisted a schoolteacher onto their shoulders and carried her down an alley. The city was en-gulfed in chaos.

Theo leaped onto the gondola platform in time to see Cess open the control box of the Suction-Flux Hydro-Debogilator. Cess grabbed the knob and turned it to the right as far as it went, well into the red zone. He pulled off the knob and threw it out the doorway.

"There!" said Cess.

"Wait!" cried Theo.

Cess grinned maliciously.

"Indeed," he said. "That's all that's left to do now, my boy."

Chapter 23
Choosing Sides and Paying the Cost

THE THROBBING HUM FROM the Suction-Flux Hydro-Debogilator had intensified to a shrieking roar. The soil around Mossville became steadily drier as the monstrous pump pulled the moisture from deep within the ground. Cracks appeared between the cobblestones of the town as the ground beneath them began to parch.

In Kook Bog, the roaring mud river at the base of the cliffs had become broader and deeper and rushed with a foaming ferocity. The swamp beneath the village rose rapidly, washing away the lowest walkways and decks. Buildings toppled into the mire as the flimsier stilts and pilings snapped like twigs against the force of the surging mud. Villagers scrambled to the highest decks and climbed upon the swaying roofs.

Cynthia, Digniggleby, Valerie, Berke, and Rudy huddled with a group of switchboard operators upon the roof of the communication gazebo.

From his vantage point over Mossville, Theo could only see what was happening in the city, but he could all too well imagine the mayhem unfolding in Kook Bog. He ran to the doorway of Cess's office.

"You'll kill them!" he cried.

Cess turned on Theo.

"Boy, I've given you an incredible opportunity here," he threatened. "Don't throw it away by making a nuisance of yourself!"

"No," said Theo. "This isn't what I want."

Cess lunged forward.

"Fine then!" he said. He straight-armed Theo hard in the chest, thrusting him back out the door onto the gondola platform. In the same motion he swung around and punched the gondola launch button in the wall.

The gondola shot off from the platform, catching Theo at an odd angle. Rather than wedging him into the seat, it knocked him crazily over the railing of the platform. Theo dangled from the platform, clutching the base of the railing as the gondola flew off.

"Blast!" said Cess. He ran to the platform and stomped at Theo's hands.

Theo hung on by one hand then the other, avoiding Cess's kicks. He swung back and forth.

Below him to the side was the maintenance catwalk for the Suction-Flux Hydro-Debogilator. He swung with all his might, angling himself as well as he could towards the catwalk. He heaved towards the catwalk just as Cess's foot came down on the tips of his fingers.

"Ow!" he cried, letting go. He swung over to the catwalk and thumped down on his chest, his feet kicking out freely under him. He grunted in pain and hoisted himself onto the catwalk.

Cess rushed to the rail of the gondola platform to see Theo racing away along the catwalk towards the towering pump.

"Blasted little monkey!" seethed Cess. He ran back into his office. He emerged with a huge blunderbuss almost as long as he was tall. He packed in a round and leveled the gun.

Theo made it across the catwalk and climbed onto the maintenance ladder of the Suction-Flux Hydro-Debogilator itself. Cess squeezed off a round but the ball went wide of the mark. It struck the metal catwalk with a shower of sparks as Theo scrambled up the ladder.

In Kook Bog, the village was being torn apart. Buildings collapsed and the decks strained against the rushing flood of mud. Villagers climbed upon makeshift rafts and anything that would float. Whole houses came loose from their pilings and floated away, their residents clinging to chimneys and gutters for dear life. The communications gazebo shuddered and creaked.

Above, through a clearing in the clouds, Valerie saw the looming arc of Suction-Flux Hydro-Debogilator. She saw something else as well.

"Look!" she shouted.

The others looked. High above, enshrouded in mist and scarcely bigger than a speck, was a figure climbing the surface of the enormous structure.

"It's Theo!" said Valerie.

"What's he doing?" said Berke.

"Son!" said Rudy. "He's trying to save us!"

The maintenance ladder was no more than a series of iron rungs welded onto the hull of the Suction-Flux Hydro-Debogilator. It extended all the way to the apex of the arc. Theo clung to the ladder and tried to resist the urge to look down. But the commotion behind him was impossible to ignore. He looked back over the catwalk and the house, where Cess stood raging on the balcony with his unwieldy firearm. Cess let off another poorly-aimed round and Theo flinched as the ball banged a dent in the iron below him.

Below, the fields and meadows around Mossville looked like a whirling green quilt. The far end of the black parabola extended into Kook Bog. From where Theo was at this height he could see the mud erupting from around the base of the enormous pump and coursing into the village. His head spun and he closed his eyes and gripped the rungs of the ladder.

He was near the peak of the arc when another blunderbuss ball struck the machine a few feet above him and a spray of water erupted from a ruptured hose. Buffeted by wind and moisture, Theo gripped the slick, wet metal of the rungs and pulled himself closer to the control box at the top of the pump. The rag around his wrist had come loose and fluttered like a tattered pink flag in the wind. The handcuff rattled against the hull of the machine. Slowly he made his way to the control box.

The control box was behind a tangle of narrow pipes and woefully inadequate-looking metal safety rails. To access the control box, Theo rested his foot against a pipe and leaned back against one of the rails, wedging himself in place. The narrow metal rail was no more than a half an inch thick and it strained under the full brunt of Theo's weight.

The control box was about five feet wide and three feet high. Theo struggled to remove the front panel which popped off suddenly and nearly caused him to lose his balance. The gunmetal rectangle fluttered into the abyss below.

Before him were the manual override controls for the Suction-Flux Hydro-Debogilator. He held his hand up to block some of the water spray so he could get a better look.

The panel was covered with hundreds of cryptically labeled switches, knobs, buttons and dials. Theo blinked. He had no idea where to begin. He remembered looking at the plans of the machine. The guide for the manual override had been missing.

He scanned the panel and racked his brain for some kind of clue. There must be some kind of logic to the controls. But he could not see it. There were far too many controls to guess at, and he could make no sense of any of them.

The water rushed over him and the screeching roar of the machine was deafening.

Valerie, Rudy, and the rest watched Theo's tiny figure at the control panel on the apex of the machine.

"Nothing's happening," said Valerie.

"Oh, dear," said Diggleby. "It's as I feared."

"What's the matter, Meriweather?" said Cynthia.

They all looked at Diggleby. He shook his head.

"He can't operate the controls," said Diggleby. "I'm no expert, but I watched them build it. It's a very complicated machine. The standard operation is difficult enough, but the manual override is impossible. Even Mr. Cess doesn't know how that works."

The group went quiet. If Theo wasn't able to operate the machine, it would all be for nothing. They would perish in the mud. And as for Theo, he would be trapped thousands of feet above the ground with no escape.

"I know how it works."

The voice came from behind them. They all turned to see its source.

The Kook Bog hermit stood before them on a large, knotty tree branch that jutted from the mud. His white hair was wild and his long beard waved in the wind. His eyes were focused and intense. Upon his left shoulder sat Buford the Toad.

Rudy gasped.

"Father!" he said.

For indeed, it was Pythagoras Promovendis himself who stood before them, the exiled inventor of the Suction-Flux Hydro-Debogilator and the unsung savior of Mossville.

Pythagoras looked at Rudy for several long moments.

"You always wanted to help me," he said. "Well, you can help me now. I need a word with that boy."

Rudy stared mutely at his long-lost father. He stared as if he were seeing an apparition.

"Now!" said Pythagoras.

Rudy snapped back to himself. He took out his palette and a pouch of substances. He gestured at Valerie to collect the twine and hooks that covered the gazebo.

"I need a connection!" he said, hurriedly mixing up his pollens.

Bugs began to swirl and collect above the surface of the mud.

Theo squeezed his eyes shut and tried to think. The pumping mechanisms of the Suction-Flux Hydro-Debogilator pounded furiously. If he did the wrong thing he would kill everyone in a single stroke. But if he did nothing, Kook Bog would be hopelessly submerged in no time. He had to do something, and fast.

Blindly, he reached towards the control panel. His hand hovered over the mess of switches and buttons.

"What am I doing?" he said out loud to himself.

Amid the roar another sound became audible. It was faint at first but became gradually louder. Theo recognized it immediately. It was the unmistakeable sound of bugs, many and near. Theo strained to look over his shoulder in the direction of the growing hum.

Behind him, a towering formation of bugs rose into the sky. Multifarious columns of insects swarmed in patterns, creating a dazzling, brightly-colored lattice.

But there was something else. Tight clusters of bugs were carrying things. Theo squinted through the mist to see. In a moment he recognized the objects. They were hooks from the Kook Bog telephone system. A long line of twine extended from one hook to the next in a broad, crazy zigzag from the ground to the sky. Theo watched in amazement as the final section of taut twine arced through the bright air toward him like the second hand of an enormous clock.

At the end of the twine was a tin can. It came to a stop within Theo's reach and he grabbed it.

"Hello!" he spoke into the can, then hastily put it to his ear.

The voice he knew only as the hermit of Kook Bog came through the line.

"Son, this is your grandfather," said the voice. "Now listen close and do as I say. I'm not in the habit of wasting my breath."

Theo blinked. For a moment he was too stunned to speak, but he caught himself quickly.

"Okay," he said.

Below, in Kook Bog, the gazebo trembled violently, but Pythagoras stood steadily. Years of living in the outer reaches of Kook Bog had left him sure footed in even the muddiest of conditions. His eyes were steely and he spoke clearly into the tin can.

"There is a three by five grid of toggles to the left of three knobs. The current settings for the toggles are: on, off, off, on, on for the first row; off, off, off, on, on for the second row; and on, on, on, on, off for the third row. Is this what you see?"

Theo frantically searched the control panel for the toggles. There were so many toggles! A three by five grid to the right, no, to the left of three knobs... Yes, there they were. He quickly recalled the pattern Pythagoras had just read out. There was no time to ask him to repeat it.

"I think that's right," said Theo.

"The second row needs to be set at: off, on, off, on, off," said Pythagoras.

Theo flipped the switches.

"Second row," he repeated, "off, on, off, off—"

"On!" corrected Pythagoras. "Off, on, off, on, off!"

Theo shook his head, flustered.

"Right, got it!" he said. "On."

"Read it back to me!" said Pythagoras.

Theo read back the pattern. At once the shrieking of the Suction-Flux Hydro-Debogilator changed tone. Spray filled the air even more thickly than before. The bugs reacted to the spray. Their formation quivered and sections of the twine went momentarily slack.

"What did you say?" said Theo. "I can't hear you!"

Cess loaded another round into his blunderbuss. On the balcony behind Cess, Bea's bugs suddenly pulled away from her. Her body tensed and reeled, fighting to keep the bugs together. The cloud of bugs around her grew sparse and shapeless one moment, then drew into tight, knotty bunches the next. Her fists clenched as she struggled to keep herself together. She floated a few feet into the air on a shifting cloud of insects. She fought frantically as one limb after the next went slack and floated powerlessly.

Throughout the city, the army of automatons struggled the same way as their bugs abandoned them and rose to join the writhing swarms above. One by one the automatons dropped limply to the ground.

At the base of the Suction-Flux Hydro-Debogilator, a massive bubble of mud rose and burst. The mud flowed more heavily than ever.

Rudy struggled to stay upright as the splashing mud rushed by on all sides of the gazebo. He dipped a twig into chemical solutions and scrawled arcane, precise diagrams on the surface of a broad, wilted petal. He sucked his mustache nervously as he watched the bugs above respond.

Behind Theo, the bugs tightened their formation and pulled the line taut. Pythagoras's voice came through the can.

"Find the aperture knob. It's below the pressure meter on the left side of the panel. It's black with a silver base. Red numbers around it."

"There are... there are two like that," said Theo.

"No there aren't!" said Pythagoras. "Silver base!"

Sure enough, only one had a silver base. The other was all black.

"Set that to the square root of the value on the pressure me-ter," said Pythagoras.

"Huh?" Theo blurted.

"What does the pressure meter say?" said Pythagoras.

"The... the one with the needle?"

"Yes! The red needle!"

There was a meter with a red needle all right, but it was vibrating so rapidly it was impossible to get a reading for it.

"It's going back and forth a lot," said Theo.

"Between what?"

"About 105 and 111," said Theo.

"Call it 108," said Pythagoras. "Set the aperture at 10.4!"

"Okay!" said Theo.

"Now all that's left is to enter the values for the shunt and to trigger the alternate output," said Pythagoras. "First of all, do you see the output nozzle at the top of the arch? Big brass flange at the base?"

Theo looked up above his head to see the massive grated nozzle at the peak of the machine. It looked like an enormous sprinkler head.

"Yeah, I see it," said Theo. "What do I need to do with it?"

"You need to stay clear of it!" said Pythagoras. "Now find the numerical key pad and enter these values. And listen good, because there's not enough time for me to say this twice!"

Pythagoras began reciting numbers. Theo frantically punched the round, mechanical number keys with one hand, steadying himself against the rushing spray with the other. He held the tin can in the crook of his neck.

"... 6, 4, 0, 0, 1, 2, 6," finished Pythagoras. "Did you get that all?"

"I think so," said Theo.

"Now just switch the release to auxiliary and stay clear," said Pythagoras.

Theo saw the knob labeled *RELEASE*. There were two labels: Main and *Auxiliary*. The arrow was pointing to *Main*.

"Okay," said Theo. He reached towards the knob.

On the balcony below, Cess steadied his blunderbuss for another shot. He squeezed the trigger and a blast rang out. The round struck the hull just inches away from Theo's head with a deafening clang. The impact jolted the machine and Theo jerked reflexively. The struts that supported the safety rail beneath him gave way and he tumbled backwards, flailing his arms. The handcuff on his wrist caught on one of the struts and he dangled helplessly.

"Got you, you little bugger!" sneered Cess.

The others saw Theo fall as well.

"Theo!" cried Valerie.

Pythagoras spoke under his breath. "Auxiliary release, boy!"

Theo summoned all his strength to pull himself up, but the harder he struggled the more the strut bent downward.

Valerie turned to Rudy. "The bugs!" she cried.

Rudy was already drawing frantically on the petal. He sucked madly on his mustache.

A cloud of gnats thickened around Theo, creating a living, flying cushion in the air. The cloud rose and Theo rose with it. He reached out as far as he could. His fingers touched the release knob. He turned it.

Water erupted from the massive nozzle in a huge, explosive torrent. The gnats dispersed in a moment, dropping Theo back to where he had been dangling at the end of the strut. The rushing water whipped him to and fro.

Water poured over Cess as he stood on his balcony, knocking him off of his feet. The house shuddered and shook. Bea's bugs abandoned her and her body toppled over the rail of the balcony. A cloud of bugs followed her down.

In Kook Bog, water poured from the sky. Everyone covered themselves in the deluge. Digniggleby turned to Pythagoras desperately.

"What's happening?" he said.

Pythagoras watched the torrents emerging from the Suction-Flux Hydro-Debogilator and raised his index finger.

"One moment..." he said.

A moment passed.

"Now," he said.

With a thunderous roar, a huge blast of mist exploded from the nozzle of the Suction-Flux Hydro-Debogilator. At once the water no longer fell downward but rather formed an enormous floating disk of moisture that extended upward and outward, spreading well beyond both Mossville and Kook Bog. The sun shone through the mist in brilliant, shifting rainbows that shimmered over the land as far as the eye could see.

In Kook Bog the mud slowed and began to subside. The clouds broke up over the bog and the sun shone brightly on the trees.

The ground in Mossville softened and bubbled. Clouds of moisture burst from the ground in puffs like steam from thick, simmering soup. The ground beneath the patent office shifted nauseatingly and gave way. The scaffolding holding up Cess's house splayed outward and folded in upon itself in a scream of twisting, scraping steel. Cables snapped and whipped the air and the elevator crumpled like cardboard. The house groaned and split clean down the middle, an explosion of glass and dust and shingles bursting from the rupture. The whole crumbling house toppled slowly and fell from its lofty perch in a spectacular, earth-shaking collapse. A monstrous cloud of dust and debris rose as the building plunged into the thickening mud, pulverized by its own weight.

Far above Theo still hung by his wrist, exhausted, from the end of the straining strut.

Valerie pointed at him and screamed.

"Help him!"

Rudy mixed pollens and drew frantically, but the bugs would not be controlled.

"I'm trying! It's all the water!" he said.

A sparse cloud of insects circled Theo aimlessly. They whirled and glided and drifted away. A purple and black-winged butterfly fluttered idly in front of Theo's nose.

The strut bent downward, the handcuff slipped free, and Theo fell.

Chapter 24
The Bugs and Their Business

FROM THE ROOF OF THE communications gazebo, Rudy, Valerie and the rest watched in horror as Theo fell.

"Theo!" cried Valerie.

"Son!" gasped Rudy.

Theo's silhouette, tiny against the blue sky, seemed to plunge for an eternity. He turned slowly head over heels in the air. Seconds passed and he rushed ever more quickly towards the earth.

He disappeared beyond the ridge. Valerie buried her face in her hands and sobbed. Rudy gaped. The palette dropped from his hands and tears welled up in his eyes.

The mud receded throughout Kook Bog. It stopped moving and the wet shine of its surface dulled. The air glittered with moisture.

Villagers and recent arrivals climbed from roofs and trees. They tested the ground with their feet before stepping cautiously onto the soft, but firm, ground.

Beyond the edge of the village, the river of mud had stopped flowing. Its ripples and eddies looked as though they had been carved into the surface of a vast slab of clay.

The people of Kook Bog congregated at the banks.

A villager stepped out cautiously and put his foot down. The ground gave slightly but supported his weight. He walked out onto the river. The crowd did the same, tentatively in pairs and threes at first and then all together as a group. When they reached the other side they began to climb up the black rock slopes towards Mossville, finding pathways as they went.

In Mossville the sun shone brightly. The moisture in the air was dissipating but rainbows still hung throughout the town.

The ground was soft but firm. The cobblestone streets had been pulled asunder by the shifting of the earth beneath them. Buildings stood at surprising angles, but for the most part they remained intact. Cess's precariously elevated home and the patent office beneath it were the only structures that had been utterly destroyed.

The house and patent office lay in a gigantic, pulverized heap, deeply embedded in a wide crater of hardening mud. The remnants of the automatons who had worked in the patent office were scattered throughout the wreckage. Broken doll heads and skeletal metal limbs poked up through the debris. Tattered scraps of burlap fluttered in the wind.

A few yards from the rim of the crater, Bea lay partially submerged in mud. A light cloud of insects still clung to her. The cloud pulsated slowly. Then, as though with great effort, it began to move around her body and head. A few more insects from the air collected around her. Aphids split off from gnats and formed a wispy but coherent stream that began to course through Bea's circulation system. Gnats clustered around her joints and moths began to accumulate around her head. She began to stir.

Unsteadily, she raised her face from the mud.

The citizens of Mossville came out of their homes and hiding places to assess the scene. At first only a few people noticed the figures appearing over the distant ridge, but soon word had spread throughout Mossville. The citizens collected on balconies and roofs to get a better look. With binoculars and telescopes, or just squinting their eyes, they watched as the mass of exiles approached from beyond the edge of the city.

As the growing crowd trudged through the still muddy fields and came into clearer view, the citizens began to register their recognition. Shouts went up throughout Mossville as fathers, mothers, aunts and uncles appeared over the hills. Long lost siblings shambled into view, black-sheep cousins and crazy godparents, caked in mud and smiling uncertainly as they trudged towards their homes. Another crowd gathered of citizens walking from the city center towards the fields to meet their returning loved ones.

Rudy, Pythagoras, Valerie, and the Dignigglebys moved among the returning exiles. But they were not looking towards the Mossville skyline. They pushed through the crowd towards the spot beneath the apex of the Suction-Flux Hydro-Debogilator in the midst of the broad muddy expanse between the ridge and Mossville.

It was Valerie who saw him first.

"Theo!" she shouted. She ran toward a gentle slope of mud beyond the edge of the crowd. Rudy and the others followed her.

Theo lay on his back, embedded in the soft earth. His mouth was open and his eyes were closed. He was not moving. Valerie fell to her knees beside him and put her ear close to his nose and mouth. No breath came. She pressed her fingers to his neck and collapsed in sobs.

Rudy also rushed to Theo's side. He touched Theo's neck and face. There was no sign of a pulse.

"Son!" he shouted.

Theo was still as a stone. Rudy buried his head in his hands. "Theo!"

Pythagoras watched from a few yards away. His face was stern but his eyes welled up with tears.

A small group of onlookers from both Mossville and Kook Bog had gathered around the group. They watched silently.

A faint buzzing sound came from behind a cluster of onlookers. The small crowd parted to let Bea through and others turned to look at her.

She was covered with mud and her purple dress was in tatters. Her porcelain head was badly chipped and cracked. She staggered weakly, close to collapse with every step. Her bugs were disorderly and sparse, and her limbs fluctuated between holding their positions and drifting limply. At moments her body seemed to float aimlessly between steps. She gripped a clump of flowers in her hands.

Valerie watched wordlessly as Bea approached and laid the clump of flowers on Theo's chest. Tears streamed down Valerie's face.

Bea knelt beside Theo and took one of the flowers from his chest. She peeled the leaves off of its stem, then crushed the leaves in her fingers until they were just a moist green powder that caked her fingers. Then she thrust her fingers deeply into Theo's mouth.

Rudy started forward to pull the strange creature from his son, but Valerie raised her hand to stop him. She stared at Bea intently. The tear stains on her cheeks had begun to dry. Something was happening.

Bea took another flower from Theo's chest. She pulled several stamens from the flower. She pushed them each as far up Theo's nostrils as she could and brushed them around, spreading their dust throughout his nasal cavity.

Rudy watched with growing fascination.

From the next flower, Bea pulled the pistil and squeezed its base until a fine clear liquid dripped out. She let several drops fall into each of Theo's eyes.

She pulled open Theo's shirt. She took the petals from the last flower and rubbed them into the skin of Theo's neck and chest.

A deeper buzzing sound became audible. Rudy looked up to see a cloud of bugs approaching.

All at once, the bugs descended upon Theo. They covered his head and flew in thick, rapid clouds into his nose and mouth. They circulated into his ears and clustered around the slits of his his closed eyes, creating a thick green eyeshadow of aphids.

The cloud of bugs pushed further into his nose and mouth and his chest rose. The cloud emerged rapidly from his nose and mouth and his chest went down. The aphids pushed his eyes open slowly. His eyes stared blankly into the sky.

Again, the cloud of bugs pushed into and out of his mouth, raising and lowering his chest. Bugs continued to course into and out of his ears and nose.

The bugs surrounded him completely, raising him out of the mud and lifting his torso a few inches above the ground.

Suddenly, Theo's eyes focused. His body thrashed and he coughed violently. The bugs dropped him to the ground with a thud and he rolled onto his hands and knees, clutching at his chest. He coughed a cloud of gnats and tried to wipe the bugs from his eyes, nose, and mouth. He gagged and spit and sneezed, and tears streamed down his red face.

Eventually the last of the bugs left him. He slumped onto his side, leaning up on one arm and heaving for breath. He looked around.

Valerie, Rudy and Pythagoras stared wide-eyed, along with the rest of the onlookers. Nobody moved a muscle for a long, long moment.

Upon a stone a few yards away a family of toads watched the scene with what appeared to be great interest.

The villagers of Kook Bog continued to spill over the ridge and into Mossville city limits. The sun shone brightly all around.

Chapter 25
A New Morning for Stationery and Soap

A STAGE WAS SET UP in the newly-cobbled town square and the townspeople thronged around it. The square was festooned with lanterns and colored paper ribbons. A banner over the stage read **MOSSVILLE SALUTES THREE GENERATIONS OF HEROES**. On stage, a band of schoolchildren played.

Theo, Rudy, and Pythagoras stood on the stage. Theo glowed with pride. Pythagoras wore a slight smile—an expression of hard-won peace. Rudy stood between them, one hand on each of their shoulders, filled with pride and love for his father and his son.

Mayor Felix, deservedly elected after a career of dedicated public service as a patent office clerk, stood at the microphone.

"Ladies and gentleman," said Felix. "Today we celebrate the righting of great wrongs, and extend the gratitude of all the hearts of Mossville to three generations of brilliant men and selfless heroes. Please join me in expressing our profound appreciation to Pythagoras, Rudolph, and Theodore Promovendis!"

The crowd erupted in applause. Valerie stood in front of the stage smiling widely. Bea stood next to her, holding her hand. Theo reached down from the stage and Valerie lifted Bea up and passed her to Theo.

Theo held Bea up for everyone to see and the crowd applauded even more jubilantly.

Meriweather Diniggleby stood proudly in front of a small shopfront on the square. A hand-painted sign in the window read *Diniggleby's Fine Bath and Office Goods*. In the window a lovingly arranged display of bath and office-related items was laid out: a typewriter mounted on a floatation device, fountain pens with scrub-brushes attached, and a wide selection of oblong soap paperweights in every color you could imagine. Cynthia Diniggleby peered out at the festivities from behind the window.

In the hills to the west, near the mud slope that once was Gurwell's barley field, Ballhatchet and Dooley stood knee deep in mud as they shoveled it into a wheelbarrow. They wore matching coveralls, crusted head to toe in dried mud. They watched the fireworks explode in the distance.

"You ever miss the old job, Dooley?" asked Ballhatchet.

Dooley thought about it for a minute.

"Not really," he said.

Ballhatchet nodded in agreement. He scratched his nose.

"Y'know, one of these days, somebody's gonna make a fortune on baby wigs," he said.

"Yeah," said Dooley.

Ballhatchet sniffed. Dooley shrugged. The two of them returned to digging.